Orbit of Strangers

Ethel Gregory

Contents

Chapter 1

"Right, I've got ten minutes before I'm expected to cast off, so get all the supplies ready by then," Leader told him in the mindhome as he left the briefing room. "Quartermaster, give me the list."

"Three months' rations, four months' water and/or purifying capsules, five months' fuel just to be safe, a Zilcn drive repair kit, and an inter-system strength communicator. Planet GU-T64A is known to cause Zilcn drive anomalies. Someone check the EVA kits and life support are in order"—Leader nodded at Artist, since he preferred avoiding other people anyway—"and someone can grab my units and gear bags. Speaker, you head to HQ and sign me off as usual. I think that's all."

Speaker gave a mental nod and peeled off from the formation, making the small extra step to remind himself not to move in sync with the rest going to the third floor. Splitting his focus, he listened to Leader assign the rest of his tasks with his usual efficiency as he turned left and headed for the elevator, greeting several Hirizcn employees with a faint smile as he passed. Since it was just him, they were less awkward than usual, and one electrician even smiled back at him. Speaker's smile widened and he broadcasted triumphantly into the mindhome. "That's another successful inter-action. One more point to being separated encouraging positive social interactions."

"I don't understand why I'm such a discon-certing sight to unattached minds," Scholar replied while loading one more zoology article into his personal unit, "but I'm glad I put the electrician at ease this way. This is why you're the Speaker and not me."

"ETA for me is five minutes. I've got the food supplies and Quartermaster is rechecking the Zilcn equipment. Socialization will have to wait until I'm back on base." Leader cocked his head in the mindhome in the way that meant not to take things too seriously, and he all sent their understanding in return.

The elevator dinged and Speaker pulled his attention back to the real world. As much as he loved focusing inward and keeping track of the rest of his movements, interacting with those outside the hive mind was hard and holding two conversations at once was distracting. As always, the person at the missions desk looked up and waved him over as the door opened, holding out the padscreen for him to sign.

Bcqu for the mission to investigate technological ruins on GU-T64A? the lady asked, the shoulders of her blue-edged uniform pulled tight with bad posture and general nervousness.

That's me, Speaker replied and reached for the pen to sign the usual waiver contracts. With half an ear, he noticed the HQ conversations falter and start up again. Really, after seven years' experience with a flawless record he would've thought everyone would be used to him receiving missions by now. There. Anything special for potential threats or excavation? I notice the mission's marked 9C for danger.

The lady took the padscreen back and flipped through the tabs before shaking her head. No, that should be fine. Fly safely through the rift.

Much obliged. Have a good day-cycle, Speaker replied and turned away, weaving through the crowd quickly enough their avoidance of him would not become too obvious. Behind him, he heard the lady mutter and check something off her list.

Speaker frowned and nudged Leader's part of the mindhome as he backtracked to the elevator and began the ascent to the launching bay. "There's got to be something I'm doing wrong. Did I miss something in the subtext again? The lady is new but I still think she's nervous of me."

Leader mentally rolled his shoulders and physically waved at Speaker as he stepped into the launching bay, calling him over to help with loading the supplies in the hold. "Their minds must be different than mine, I suppose. Perhaps acting in synchrony is something they reserve for being in private? Either that or I am the first and only hive minded explorer in Hirizcn. Don't let it get you down, though. GU-T64A and its mysterious cndrids await."

"And the blue citrus!" Scholar interjected, bumping mental shoulders and physically hurrying out of the cockpit to balance the drive repair kit Speaker was lifting. "If I complete objective 1 quickly, I have leave to collect samples to bring back to the lab! My theory is that it's a close relative of the Libet lemon."

Speaker smirked in the real and internal worlds, taking the last package and heading to the copilot's seat to be Artist's liaison during liftoff. "You know I'll all help myself get as much exploration time as possible. I deserve it after such a long time on base! My socialization project can wait. I know my mental bonds are sufficient for my emotional health." He all shared internal glances and basked in understanding and excitement for the coming trip.

All hatches sealed. Bcqu, prepare for liftoff. All of him snapped to attention in the real world and buckled into his seats, sliding back into synchrony. His eyes scanned the readouts, watching all systems come online, no problems detected. Artist's fingers stitched together his course as Quartermaster crunched the numbers and Scholar checked the cargo. Leader gave him the signal and Speaker leaned forward into the intercom:

Bcqu ready. Launching in 5, 4, 3, 2, 1.

The trip to GU-T64A only took 4 hours through 6th-level dimensional rift. However, the Zilcn drive refused to exit to normal space at the specified point and so they overshot by a couple parsecs. After three more tries and increasing frustration from all angles of the mindhome, he all eventually settled on only entering 1st-level dimensional rift and traveling for 12 more hours, bringing their total travel time to one full day-cycle.

"How did that freelance engineer get here in the first place?" Artist complained, seat tilted fully back and arm over his face. "This is more than 'mild Zilcn drive interference'. This is 'nearly impossible to get to'!"

He all groaned in agreement, cranky and tired from hours of crunching numbers and troubleshooting the interference in the Zilcn drive. There'd been enough turbulence and astronavigation calculations that he'd forgone usual sleep shifts so he could devote all his mind to successfully arriving at the planet.

"The suspected importance of these ancient robots better be worth our time," Quartermaster said grimly, still typing equations into the displays in the physical cockpit. "With my updated calculations there is a 67% chance our drive will fail once we exit rift. The engineer was incredibly lucky to be able to leave at all. This is why I packed so many additional supplies."

All of him turned to stare at Quartermaster, which only made it more awkward when Quartermaster broke synchrony to stop looking at himself. The drive hummed in the silence as he slowly dragged his hand through his spiky copper hair. "I didn't mention that before, did I?"

"You never brought that to the mindhome," Speaker confirmed, spreading his hands with the understanding tilt to preempt any frustration. "Undirected thoughts don't mix, remember?"

Rather than answer directly, Quartermaster groaned and buried his physical face in his hands, withdrawing from the mindhome. He all stopped staring and politely turned back to reading downloaded articles, attempting sleep, and monitoring his course.

Twenty minutes passed by in comfortable silence before Leader called for all his attention. "Exit in 10. 1st-level pings indicate a ship entered normal space 37 hours ago. I'll land immediately and Scholar and I will attempt to make contact with the freelancer. The rest of me divide jobs as you see fit."

"Don't you want me to talk to the engineer?" Speaker frowned while he packed up the scraps from his late supper. Scholar abandoned his article to join him, his part of the mindhome just barely sending Speaker the gist of his thoughts. All previous data on the blue citrus and its known planets, as well as more research on lemons and the pull of excitement. He sent a knowing nudge back.

Leader mentally shook his head. "I'll do it. You need to set up camp and sleep. I'm not taking remedial courses again." He pushed concern and the many posters of self-care and sleep schedules they had to memorize. He all wrinkled his physical noses in unison.

Remember to be verbal. Speaker snickered even as he all startled at the sudden speech. The rest of him really had to get used to voices on missions, even if silence was usefully safer. His career contract said to 'aspire to be ready for every situation', after all.

I'm only funny sometimes, Quartermaster said and rolled his all eyes. That Speaker's sleep was definitely recommended was left unsaid, even in the mindhome. Piloting difficulties always exacerbated his sensitivity to disturbed circadian rhythms. "By the way, exit in 15 seconds so strap in." Speaker acknowledged he was feeling a little mischievous and sent a nonverbal promise to settle down as he and Scholar buckled back into his seats.

Exit, thankfully, was smooth, and atmospheric entry was textbook simulation level. GU-T64A was an excellent temperate planet with standing water and luscious foliage, despite the unusual makeup and occasional solar storms. The ongoing theory was that the ancient civilization had terraformed the planet for human usage before disappearing to wherever they had disappeared to. Speaker and Scholar watched raptly as the rest of him circled over the rainforest, searching for a place to land, engines thrumming and wind buffeting the trees as they passed. With all the biodiversity here, it was a wonder Hirizcn hadn't sent a team to properly survey the flora and fauna earlier.

"I can't wait to begin a thorough documentation," Scholar said, quiet awe muffling all other thoughts in the mindhome. "It's beautiful."

It was. As he approached the city's ruins, taking advantage of air resistance for deceleration, brilliant spires of green pierced through the treetops, forgoing protection entirely to focus on hyperefficient photosynthesis. Huge, frond-like leaves tufted below, creating a dense canopy that Artist was itching to sample. Was the wax-like sheen a function of the light, or did it serve to funnel water down into the undergrowth? Were the ferns he could see parasitic, or did they merely grow on the main trees? How many species of frond trees would he find in this square kilometer alone?

Quartermaster finally found a place to nestle his ship without compromising the ruins, expertly alighting in a clearing with a fallen tree. With a deft tilt, he balanced the right edge on the tree and the left on the ground, creating a lean-to and saving him all half the job of making camp.

"Thanks for the idea, Artist," Leader said as the engines fell silent and he all unbuckled to change into exploration suits. He all sent his sense of gratitude and Speaker reached over to physically shake Artist more awake so he could go out the door. "I'll hopefully track down the engineer immediately and then I can relax."

He filed out of the ship and did a few stretches to test GU-T64A's gravity, craning his necks to get a good survey of the clearing and noting the high, constant insect whine every rainforest seemed to have. Leader and Scholar broke synchrony and headed north toward the city ruins, where the freelance engineer's camp was hypothesized to be. The rest of him set about unpacking the pertinent containers, constructing a weatherproof shelter, and testing the atmosphere for any problematic pathogens.

Artist was practically asleep on his feet and kept bleeding his tiredness through the mindhome, making it hard for Speaker to focus. Quartermaster took Leader's place in directing synchrony and worked with Speaker to keep prodding Artist as they laid out containers and affixed moldable insulation to the improvised walls. None of him thought very much, comfortable to sit in the mindhome and listen to the quiet buzz of Leader and Scholar picking their way through the dense undergrowth.

By the time the shelter was erected and most of his belongings were unpacked, Leader and Scholar had reached the city ruins and begun searching for heat signatures. There were surprisingly few false positives and all of him paused to wonder at the quietly still-functional animal deterrent technology scattered throughout the yellowed buildings.

A thump startled all of him into jumping and a camouflage-patterned man flew over the side of a terrace and rolled into the opposite wall. He hit it with a thump and a wheezed curse, then scrambled to his feet, dripping wet and leaving a large wet spatter on the wall. Upon catching sight of the Hirizcn-blue uniform he wore, the man growled, How many times do I have to tell you? I am not going to join your weasel-brained corporation. Stop trying to hire me.

I am not here to hire you. Hirizcn got word of an interesting cndrid you found in these ruins. We would like to see your analysis of its code, Leader said evenly, stashing his machete in sync with Scholar. Speaker absently moved his hand along the same path.

Like deathwaste am I going to hand over my hard-won data to you bloodsucking exploration companies. Go take apart an cndrid yourself. The man spat into his hand and slicked his hair out of his face. He all internally winced and noted that the microbes in the water here were likely not life-threatening, even if the water was not potable.

"Quartermaster, go find his camp and search it for a data drive," Leader said without taking his physical gaze off the engineer. Quartermaster immediately picked up his pack and headed into the undergrowth, out of Speaker's physical sight.

Oh no. "Are you sure that's wise?" Speaker butted in before Leader could verbalize his next thoughts. "That would be a disrespect of privacy and he is already hostile enough to us."

Leader waved his hand dismissively in the mindhome. "Our mission's primary objective is to obtain this information, and the engineer need not know we searched his belongings."

Speaker's intuition still revolted, so he pushed his misgivings outward and said, "Leader... You know I'm the Speaker. I think I shouldn't do this."

Leader turned to him in the mindhome and put a hand on his shoulder. "I am secondary Speaker and I think we should at least keep all options open. You need to go to sleep. Stop hovering so close." In the real world, he said, We would appreciate being able to work with you and can compensate you for this information. The encryption on these cndrids are impressive and you are the first to begin to decipher the data. Would you agree to signing a one-time contract so we can decipher the cndrid's secrets together?

That was exactly the wrong thing to say to someone so obviously defensive. Speaker slammed his head into his physical palm and groaned, "Leader, you're just making things worse. Let me tell you what to say, please."

"I found the base," Quartermaster interjected. "Should I go to investigate or not?"

"Do it," Leader said decisively and turned to Speaker. "Go to sleep."

Speaker wrinkled his mental and physical nose and laid down beside Artist in the tent. He grumbled undirected complaints into his corner of the mindhome and attempted to force his thoughts away from the interesting interaction. He knew what he was doing, even if he didn't fully agree with himself, and if worse came to worst he had enough supplies and skill to handle the consequences. Leader had better not blow the mission before he got started, though.

He pushed out the input from other corners of the mindhome and relaxed all the muscles in his body. Leaves rustled in the breeze outside and the call of some avian mingled with the ever-present buzz of insects. Speaker let his thoughts go fuzzy and drift into dozing, trusting the rest of him to do his thing.

Chapter 2

A jolt of pure adrenaline forked across the mindhome and launched him into wakefulness. "MEDEY! The engineer is fleeing, presumably toward his ship. Speaker, head south-south-west and disable his ship controls. Artist, rendezvous with Scholar and sweep the eastern ruins."

Speaker and Artist shared a charged glance and ducked out of the shelter, sealing the entrance and snatching a travel kit each. "Status? Why is he running? Quartermaster, did you find his camp yet?" Speaker asked while rifling through their containers for a heat sensor and a remote drone. Sleep still clung to him in rags and he shook his physical head hard. What was the point of sleeping if he had to get up and hunt the engineer down anyway?

"The engineer had some hidden security measures and I set off an alarm approaching his remote camp. He was alerted and blew up at Leader and Scholar before haring off into the jungle. I did not obtain the cndrid data." Quartermaster said chagrined, his corner of the mindhome rippling with snatches of the ongoing map of the area and his current surroundings.

"I told me all so! This is why I should listen when I have objections!" Speaker spat and pushed a leaf from his face. "Now my secondary recruiting objective is as good as ruined. When interacting with other people, I must take their values into account."

Leader sent acknowledgment and he all slipped into focus on his individual tasks, sending live updates and coordinating without words. This was what made him the most intimidating explorer in Hirizcn; operations with complex, time-sensitive coordination was his specialty.

Speaker consulted Quartermaster's mental map and compared it with the feed on his heat sensor. Close enough. He activated the remote drone and piloted it above the canopy to get a space-eye view of the area. Even if the engineer had access to advanced camouflage technology, there were few places for a ship to land within reasonable distance from the city ruins. A particularly strong gust of wind knocked his drone sideways, skewing the feed for a moment and drawing his attention to a suspiciously shaped rock half a kilometer away.

"I think I've got a lock on his ship. Should I stake it out or focus on hacking his systems?" he reported. The drone got stuck on one of the enormous chlorophyll spikes and he had to jerk the controller around a few times. He all would be itching to analyze those more thoroughly once this dratted data retrieval mission was over. Why couldn't Leader have adjusted for the engineer's hostility at all?

"Might as well hack. I didn't find anything at the temporary camp by the ruins so the cndrid is likely in his ship, and I am closing in on the engineer's position." Scholar lit up the mental map with approximations of everyone's location. Leader shifted focus only long enough to give a mental nod, and the mindhome shifted to accommodate all his visual input. Trees, padscreen data, and his faces flashed from all corners as he all worked to integrate the newest information.

"Right." Speaker withdrew from the mindhome and blinked a few times to recenter himself. When he was this separated and focused on diverse tasks, it always took him a moment to remember his physical surroundings, even though the rest of him seemed to have no trouble adjusting. He let the drone fall into his outstretched hand and deactivated it, restarting his jog through the jungle.

The rock was on a shelf halfway up a hill that was a pain to climb on short notice. Speaker had to take a moment to attach the drone to his pack and change the setting on his all-purpose boots before tackling the steep red slopes. The ground was mostly clay and he noted the area did not conform to the usual erosion formations; he'd have to keep that in mind when he read the cndrid's information. There were only a few recorded civilizations with this level of technology, and none of them favored unnecessary terraforming.

He slowed and briefly circled the ship from above before deciding that setting off further alarms wouldn't make the situation any worse. Sliding down, he released a localized EMP and hurriedly set about disabling the power source for the engines and Zilcn drive. He checked the mindhome for an update on the engineer and winced from the rest of his annoyance. He had set off another bevy of alarms, and the engineer had picked up his pace significantly, so the situation had gotten worse.

If the rest of him didn't manage to pin the engineer down, he'd arrive to stop him shortly. Speaker pried open the ship's door and conducted a lightning search of the interior. It was a standard passenger class with copious modifications for speed, efficiency, and interestingly, stealth. Most rooms were dedicated to work and comfort with few personal effects. There—a clearly foreign cndrid made of yellowed metal and plugged into a large monitor. Speaker shrugged off his travel pack and connected the Hirizcn standard virus to start working on the encryption. Like he'd suspected, the cndrid ran on an EMP-shielded private power system.

Another alarm went off, the ship's systems this time. Speaker hammered the nearest speaker silent, checked the encryption progress, and began cutting through the internal firewalls. The freelancer had ingenious defenses, but his hardware couldn't stand against the well-oiled knowledge and experience his career at Hirizcn had given him. Speaker had to pull from Quartermaster's specialized hacking knowledge, though. It was really too bad Leader had botched the recruitment objective of his mission.

The virus cracked the encryption and lines of code rapidly scrolled down the monitor. Standard operating procedures, factory preset commands, voice-activated directives, a warning about outdated technology, instructions for activating a temporal stasis field for space travel—!

A thump and a swear alerted him he was out of time. Speaker slammed a data chip into the connection slot and entered the command to copy everything over. Whipping out his machete, ran to the cockpit and took a defensive stance in front of the controls.

The engineer flung himself through the entrance, blood dripping from a slash on his face and some kind of heavily modified pistol in his hands. He trained the weapon on Speaker immediately and heaved the door shut with his shoulder. Get out of my ship, copyright-thieving leech! How many of you are there?

"Speaker, the engineer just entered the ship. I'll be there in 30 seconds. Don't let him take off." Leader's voice broke through his concentration, carrying the impression of channeled chaos in the rest of the mindhome.

"Acknowledged." He just had to stall without being shot with potentially lethal modified bullets. Talking was his specialty. He had to calm this situation down. He lowered his machete and raised one hand in the galactic peace gesture. I won't attack if you don't. I only know how to use this in self defense.

Get out of my ship. This is private property and you are violating seventy-one terms of the Agatian Document of Civil Rights. I won't ask twice. He gestured with his gun and warmed the barrel up to an ominously glowing blue.

Deescalate, deescalate. Speaker lowered his machete further and affected an embarrassed grimace. He hoped it was not intimidating. I'm sorry about that. I can be a bit of an arrogant jerk sometimes.

Like he hoped, the admission caught the engineer wrong-footed. You— There's no way you could've arrived here before I did. You're that hivemind abomination made by Sicntia, aren't you? I know you're more than capable of decoding the cndrid code. Leave me alone and do the work yourselves for once rather than stealing it off of those trying to make a living apart from your precious corporations.

"I'm surrounding the ship. Speaker, did you let off an EMP? I can't remotely access the ship's systems," Scholar reported and nudged him in the mindhome.

Startled, Speaker lost track of the inoffensive answer he was trying to formulate and moved in synchrony with Artist's stumble somewhere outside the ship. The sudden movement pulled him from the doorway, and the engineer shoved him aside to lunge for the manual restart for the ship's power. His verbal shout mixed with the chaos inside and outside the mindhome as the engines stuttered to life and jerked the ship into the air, throwing all of him off of his feet.

Speaker forced himself from synchrony to roll and snatch his machete away from his face, sheathing it before it could cut anyone's arm open. "What are you doing?" he yelled before realizing he'd forgotten to speak aloud. *What are you doing? If you're going to kidnap part of me at least make sure I'm strapped in and won't break my neck!*

As long as I'm flying in atmosphere you can't attempt to hijack me and neither can your comrades down below, the engineer growled and hooked his leg under a seat arm as he threw the ship into a barrel roll. *I'll deal with you later.*

"This guy is insane!" Artist yelled as Speaker abandoned his attempt to get into a seat and curled into the safety position. Something crashed into his back, then his crossed arms, and ominous crunching noises came from somewhere in the back. If that was the priceless cndrid and its partially-deciphered time stasis information, he all would murder this safety-flaunting engineer in his bunk, mission or no mission.

The engine stalled. Speaker's stomach flew up with his feet as they lost momentum and began to fall. *Screw it all.* Pushing aside his adrenaline as best as he could and blocking out the rest of his extraneous input, Speaker grabbed the nearest zero-g handholds and shot himself toward the control panel. The engineer whirled, drawing his—"Is he really going to insist on having a close quarters gun fight right now?"—weapon and charging it up despite the ship currently being in freefall.

Speaker turned his shoulder forward and rammed into the engineer, sending them both sprawling over the controls. His head smacked into the engineer's wet outfit and he scrambled for the emergency autopilot. What was their altitude now? How far did they have before they hit the treeline? Quartermaster shouted something about an emergency landing but Speaker had no time to process as the engineer shoved an elbow in his gut.

Distress signal detected. Beginning countdown to blink.

Who is— The engineer jerked away from Speaker's attempted disarming wrist twist and brought his gun to face the automated voice.

Speaker took the moment to check altitude—1.7km and dropping, not good—and pulled the lever. The ship's alarm began to sound as manual controls went into lockdown and oxygen and portable EVA field generators popped out from under the dashboard. "Autopilot activated!" he called into the mindhome and risked a look at what had the engineer's attention.

The half-gutted cndrid swung on the handle it was gripping as the backup generator kicked into gear and Speaker and the engineer slammed into the floor from the ending freefall. Red-flickering plasma emanated from its strange liquid core, shooting out in arcs that were not stable by any theory Speaker knew in the physics books. How was it even partially functional? Wires were still trailing behind it, complete with welded access panels!

Whatever blink is, it's likely as an unstable black hole to kill us if it runs that protocol now, the engineer hissed and whipped his gun back into position off the floor. Do I have to do all the work or do you miraculously have some knowledge that you managed to absorb in the ten seconds you've gotten to study this thing?

Emergency landing in 10 seconds. Please buckle your seat-belts, the ship's computer announced over Speaker's wildly darting thoughts. The shouting in the mindhome trampled any sent idea before he could catch a hold of it and the panic meant he could not block the rest of himself out. Now was not the time to freeze up! Shaking his physical head furiously, he pulled himself up on a seat and threw the only object he had on hand.

As his machete whirled through the air, the ship's engine sputtered again and shut off. Blink activated, the cndrid said smugly as sudden weight filled Speaker's limbs and the Zilcn drive roared into life.

Chapter 3

Nothing.

He was ripped apart from himself and flung bleeding into the void. All sense of awareness fractured and the emptiness of deep space feasted on his rapidly disintegrating form. Any thought he had spun out into the silence and was swallowed, an echo stifled with no friendly mind to bounce the thought back.

He clung to the remnants of his essence with what body he had, but every attempt to clench his fingers only further yanked his unraveling strands deeper into the darkness. It was death, collapsing, slow, and agonizing death.

He floated in the void. The bleeding of his soul had slowed but he could not muster any awareness or thought beyond the sensation of pain. The strands that had been yanked from him had long since disappeared into the vastness, perhaps burnt in the heart of some cold distant star. Emptiness throbbed in his mind as silent cries echoed outward and were lost with no reply.

Time existed but he did not track its passing, too lost in the unending lack of himself. Where am I? Where am I? Where am

I? poured in ceaseless repeat from lips made stiff and dry from crusted blood. The darkness was everywhere, and no matter where he turned he was alone in the vastness of space. He grasped for thoughts and knowledge but they were lost in the emptiness of his spirit.

The persistent ticking of a clock and the steady whishing of forced ventilation slowly pulled Speaker from the void. He kept his eyes closed and body still, teetering between wanting to in-vestigate his surroundings or to fall back into the darkness. Artist would— But no, he had no Artist now and the rest of him was gone. He folded in on himself and nearly lost awareness in the horror of his empty mind.

The mindhome did not even have ruins.

Emotions strangled his throat and he choked as air was forced into his lungs. His hands twitched uselessly like when he had first been formed and the sensation of an oxygen mask burned on the contours of his face. He was on a ventilator, and the uncomfortable needle of an IV prickled in his left arm. Who had rescued him and forced him to live through the end of his existence? Why couldn't they have let him languish and follow the rest of himself in peace?

Stumbling in the darkness yielded nothing but agony as cry after cry stuttered in his mind and died before it could leave his physical throat. He could not ask for help in this state, and did he even want to? The injury was too great, and no one outside of himself could heal this pain anyway. Distantly he wondered whether he was going into shock, and if that even applied when the shock was the loss of his mind rather than the loss of one or more of his limbs. Hirizcn had trained him for many scenarios, but nothing could have prepared him for losing himself.

Footstep vibrations and the telltale hiss of a sliding door made him reconsider his decision to open his eyes. He struggled a moment, disoriented without the direction of the mindhome to synchronize and guide him. The sudden input of a cold hand on his forehead shocked him into a startle response and his eyes fluttered open, feeble as he was.

A strangely rounded face lit up at his response and began speaking with slowly enunciated words as she removed her hand and began tending to the various devices attached to his body. It was not standard Gatik, nor even any of the major lingua franca also in use in less civilized corners of the galaxy. He seized onto the unfamiliar puzzle with all the desperation of the blood he could still taste floating in the void.

Lots of voiced consonants, long phrases, and the occasional word that sounded almost like one he should understand, all spoken in a soothing tone. She was likely attempting to explain the situation to him... Come to think of, where was the excuse of an engineer who caused his death in the first place? How far had the "blink" taken him?

Leader would know. Quartermaster would have already drawn up so many more implications from his current situation and Scholar would... Scholar would... That brief foray into ancient linguistics...

The void where the mindhome used to be swallowed him.

He had found that the only way to escape the crushing pressure of the void was to ground himself in his physical reality. His body still floundered without the mindhome to direct his movements, but by pulling on long-dormant memories he had rediscovered the trick, at least for unpressured motions. Several nurses had come and gone on quiet feet, but he had not turned to acknowledge them; even the thought of attempting to understand other minds had him shuddering and floundering away from the yawning tatters of his own. He may have been the part called Speaker, but he was a shadow of himself without the constant support and reflection inside the mindhome. Simply choosing to continue his existence was a battle he hardly had the strength to fight.

Food was difficult. Every unfamiliar texture and nuance reminded him of this or that fascination of Scholar's, and he had to constantly jerk himself back from reaching for Artist's inspiration, or Leader's input, or Quartermaster's instructions on what to do next. Any attempt to pull something from the mindhome sent him spiraling into the darkness without fail. At this point he estimated that he had spent weeks lying insensible in bed, and he feared for his muscle mass when he gathered the strength to attempt to rise and walk forward into life again. At least the ventilator and most of the invasive stopgap measures were gone.

The door hissed open once more and a set of boots clomped forward and hesitated on the threshold. He tightened his grip on his steadily dulling hair and redoubled his mantra for both grounding and grieving. Where am I, where am I, whereamIwhereamIwhereamIwhereamI—

A throat cleared and a stab of fury caused a hitch in his words. Why was the engineer murderer here? Was he going to scoff or gloat over the depth of his torment?

Uh, hey. Cloth rustled and the engineer growled as something sloshed and splashed onto the floor. They told me you've been having a hard time.

"A hard time." Did it even count as an inner monologue if there was no longer any mindhome to push a response to his choking words?

Said something about the shock of ripping a hivemind away from itself, and that social interaction is supposed to be good for you. Apparently they're experts in such things. They all speak some demented form of ancient English or some nonsense, so I'm here to be the translator or whatever to let you know what's going on.

He closed his eyes and curled tighter, caught between equally vivid pulsing emotions. It was the engineer's mission that led to his death, which could even be argued to be murder; his death-courting decision to attempt to escape on his ship; and his rogue cndrid that caused the "blink" that killed him. The moment of separation loomed in his memory and fire sparked, but when no response came from the darkness the action died in the mindhome. The rest of him would have wanted to gather all information and finally learn more about his captors and circumstances, and he was all that was left. He had no strength to take revenge on the engineer anyway.

A slurp and a long, drawn out sigh. We're 10,000 lightyears away in the Persius arm of the Milky Way galaxy, kid. Welcome to Dawi, inventors of another form of FTL travel and secret-hoarding misers who won't let us go home. Turns out they left the ruins on all those planets in the Plciadcs because they didn't like our civilization becoming next door neighbors.

Kid? He was maturationally twenty-six and an accoladed explorer to boot. Why was the engineer calling him a child when they were likely the same age? Was it some cultural quirk he no longer knew because the knowledge was lost along with the rest of himself? He inhaled sharply and forced his focus onto the cold comfort of his endless mantra.

You going to talk to me at all? I might hate your guts as one of those blood-sucking conglomeration employees, but the two of us are going to have to stick together if we ever want to figure out a way to steal a ship and get back into our own corner of the galaxy. With the way Zilcn drives are failing there's no way any Gatik spaceships will even touch the dust of this arm within our lifetimes.

You shouldn't know that. The words escaped his mouth before he had time to filter them, the distress at the confidential information leak flowing outward since there was no mindhome to broadcast it in.

The engineer barked laughter, short, sharp, and bitter. Oh I know that. There's a reason I have no trust in your precious corporations. Monopolies don't have a good way of innovating new answers.

The engineer's implications floated out of his grasp, leaving him frustrated with the lack in everything without the rest of himself. His mind hurt from the effort of not reaching out into the void. He moved his hands over his face and took a halting breath. Filter for only the salient points for now, since he was apparently incapable of anything else. Trapped beyond the range for Zilcn drive technology with no way home. An offer to work together. Did he want that?

"It would benefit the secondary mission objective," he whispered into the void, opening and closing his mental fingers, leaning both into the void and away. "That's what Leader would say."

No echo returned, no whispers or comments showing him another view emerged from the darkness.

He let himself fall silent and rubbed his temples, physically staring at the cream wall in front of him rather than the void. He was far, far away and unable to report to Hirizcn, let alone complete the mission. What was the point? What was the point of anything at all?

The engineer shifted and took another slurp of his drink. Look, I can't pretend to know what you're going through. But you're going to have to work with me here. Give me an answer, whether it's yes or no or I need more time to think about it. I've got my own plans to make based on what you say.

A whine escaped his clenched teeth. The darkness was closing in on him, swallowing every thought he couldn't manage to stop passively broadcasting. What was the question again? Be verbal. Just like he'd told him all before— Wait, no, back away from the void, there weren't going to be any answers there. Speak aloud. What... What was the question?

The engineer hissed. Blow my gate, kid, just how bad off are you? Never mind, don't answer that. Boots clunked and his back stiffened as the engineer's shadow fell and mysterious noises emanated from the direction of the remaining medical equipment.

You'll break something... he managed to verbalize, though the end of his sentence died in his throat. "Protocol demands only licensed medical professionals should mess with anything touching one of me, and this situation isn't dire enough to count as an emergency."

Was it, though? Most of him had been killed and he was barely strong enough to remain lucid, let alone hold an intelligent conversation. He shuddered with his full body and let himself scream into the void. How he wished Leader, or Quartermaster, or any one of him was here! Anything to make the emptiness seem a little less alone.

He stopped wallowing a little when he recognized the fuzzed awareness of a painkiller kicking in and turned his head to actually look at the engineer for the first time. The man's face was cleaner shaven and sharper than he remembered and his shirt was dark, presumably from the spill he heard earlier. Apparently the engineer knew something about how to operate this civilization's medical equipment. He licked his lips and forced himself to continue the conversation. You asked me a question, didn't you?

Yes. Are you sure you don't want to try to sleep it off first? I don't want an answer from someone who can't think clearly.

It was good reasoning, so he took a moment to center himself, examining his own awareness and coherence compared to the memories he hadn't lost in the void. His mind and heart ached, but unfortunately that was not something that would resolve with a good night's sleep. Emotional decisions were often unadvisable, Scholar would caution him here, but right now he was feeling more like Artist and just wanted to get the external human interaction over with. No. Just tell me.

An emotion too quick to parse flashed across the engineer's face. Alright. Nevertheless, his stance hardened and his words were brief and sharp, despite the casual tone in which he said them. Will you help me break their technology, steal one of this civilization's insane passenger ships, and get back into our part of the galaxy?

"I'm hardly capable of doing anything right now," he laughed, weak and warbling, curling into himself and trying to shut out the loud silence from the void. Only after an awkward physical pause did he realize he never verbalized his response. He swallowed and cleared his throat, but hesitated as he thought over again what he was going to say.

After all, what was the point of trying to convince the engineer that he was useless? He had already seen his weakness, and because of their situation he had no other options. Working together was the most feasible method to get back. He closed his eyes. He had a duty to return to Hirizcn and report— and report— and report his deaths, that he was the only one left. He should. Yes.

Good to work with you then. I'm Huras. What's your name? He opened his eyes to see the engineer holding a hand out as if to shake on the deal, eyebrows for once not tilted in dislike.

The atmosphere sucked out of his lungs, and for a moment all he could see was the darkness where Artist and Scholar and Quartermaster and Leader were not. He knew the correct answer, but his being revolted at the thought of trying to bear his name alone. He was nothing compared to the rest of himself. Bitterly, he ignored the pressure building in his eyes and turned to face the cold, blank wall. I'm no one, not any more.

CHAPTER 4

Now that this civilization's doctors had seen him interact once with Huras, they were insistent on never leaving him alone for long. Today he struggled to keep himself present as a psychologist whose name he hadn't caught yet was attempting to examine him with the engineer as a proxy. They had been stuck for ten minutes on the question of his name, but the psychologist still insisted on trying to explain around some kind of translation error.

Huras looked down at his padcreen's text-to-speech transcription, squinted as he mouthed the ancient English words, and finally made eye contact with his latest exceedingly loose translation. She says that it's great you want to distinguish yourself from the collective, but you do need a name, even a temporary one.

No, he said, clear and flat. He looked down to his hands and clenched the burnt ochre stress ball they had given him, trying not to fall back into the void. Quartermaster would scold him right now for being so sentimental, but he needed some way of coping while he grieved. He knew that he once read some psychology articles talking about that. Whether there were healthier responses was something he had lost to the void.

No, Huras sighed and let the padscreen translate into English so the psychologist could translate it to whatever language her civilization had. She frowned and spoke again, tone low and full of concern.

Frustration rose in him and he gave the stress ball another vindictive squeeze. He should be able to translate the padscreen himself. Scholar had taken an entire degree on ancient languages and drilled him all in all its various forms of writing. He should be able to gather himself and explain that he's not trying to distinguish himself from anything, and that it was insulting to keep saying so. He should be able to process his emotions in peace without having this clunky examination that had both the psychologist and Huras looking at him with ever-increasing levels of pity. But the rest of him was dead and there was a trap instead of a mindhome, and he was helpless.

Huras read the latest message and rolled his eyes, shifting and pulling up a knee to rest his chin on. Look, kid, just do us a favor and give her a name so we can move on already.

I'm not a kid, he snapped, emotions bleeding in the mindhome and finding no vent except his words. I don't need your condescension.

Then stop acting like one, Huras said, adjusting his mottled gray shirt and raising one eyebrow. You're just making things harder for everyone.

Superheated gas rose inside of him and suddenly his mind was too small to hold his tears any more. You don't understand! I can hardly string two thoughts together without risking unconsciousness and the rest of me is dead. If you're not going to let me recover, take your pity and leave. There's nothing left for me back there, anyway.

Hey—

I don't want to hear it! You killed me. You are a murderer. Get out.

His shoulders convulsed with the weight of his isolation and he abandoned his position to curl into a ball. The psychologist said something sharp to Huras, and after a tense pause, a chair scraped and Huras's boots clomped out the door. He fought back the void with the force of his agony, vaguely horrified at the intensity of his outburst.

The mattress crinkled as the psychologist sat beside him. Her strange, lyrical voice murmured comforting words as she put a hand on his back. His sobs froze for a moment at the unexpected contact. The pressure and shape of her hand was all wrong, nothing like the times he all had tried to bring Artist out of meltdowns when he was young. He wasn't supposed to break down like this, not outside the mindhome and not in front of others, but he couldn't hold it inside any longer when echoes were swallowed in the void instead of returning understanding.

Everything was wrong and nothing would be right ever again. He was going to spend the rest of his life alone and not understood because he's far too old and broken to attempt forming himself with a full mindhome again. Humans were social creatures, he remembered that much from his studies. How would he form emotional connections now?

His heart hurt and his head throbbed, and he could feel the void prodding at the loose strands of his mind. He curled tighter and drew himself inward, attempting to catch each strand and keep himself from unravelling. A memory of breathing exercises surfaced and he seized it, funneling all his attention into regulating his sobs.

Soft singing filtered into his focus, and he realized the psychologist had graduated from attempting to provide physical comfort. She was surprisingly on pitch for a civilization whose tuning system should be different from his, but further analysis and interest took far more mental effort than he could spare.

He was completely alone. Somehow, he would have to find a way to heal from this crippling injury and learn how to function like a non-hiveminded person. He'd have to find a way to live with the ever-present void in his mind and the silence whenever he wanted to process his emotions. The prospect threatened to crush him, and he focused his breathing and thought of the most beautiful night skies instead.

Astronomy had never been his favorite subject, but when he all got tired of studying and categorizing endless new or variant species and documenting landforms, he would slow down a moment and look up at the stars. So many held further exploration opportunities where the wonder of discovery was not dampened by the onslaught of logistics, and the concept of them fascinated each of him in its own right.

Leader always thought of the constellations and how the same stars told a different set of stories depending on which planets you viewed them from. Quartermaster watched the great expanses and sighed at the immense space and distance and his insignificance compared to the size of it all. Scholar alternately categorized visible stars by energy spectrum or joined one of the others in his musings. Artist heard the music of the cosmos and listened in simple adoration.

He saw the dots of light in his mind's eye and wondered if hope was how stars did not suffocate in the void.

The psychologist was uttering a refrain now, clearly a mantra of some sort. After a moment, he started and realized the song was in English. Several lines traced by, and he began to mentally translate concepts before catching himself and pulling back from the void where Scholar's knowledge had been. The song was something about a ferry and sailing beyond. He'd have to content himself with that.

By now the throes of his fury had passed and he was left with a low, simmering, murky ache. Shakily, he wiped his face on his sleeve—not his uniform, but at least they had replaced it with soft blue clothes—and sat up. The psychologist trailed off and patted him one last time, tone clearly asking if he felt better. He sent her a wan smile before realizing he had to replicate it physically, resolutely refusing to let himself feel the accompanying toll of despair.

She murmured a phrase and stood, placing her hands on his shoulders and touching her forehead to his. Again, he blanked, torn between pulling back or accepting whatever cultural gesture this was. In the end, it didn't matter, as by the time he stopped himself from sending a panicked request to Leader the psychologist had pulled away.

Kanado purim, she said, and for the first time he saw her dark eyes filled with kindness and not condescending pity. She put a hand to her heart and dipped her head. Ai Tzeldea.

He waited a moment, and she repeated the phrase. Ai Tzeldea. If that was based off of ancient English, that meant... At last, the knowledge didn't escape him and he understood. Nais miit u, he whispered back, sinuses clogged with the inevitable snot after tears. Tzeldea.

Chapter 5

Huras returned to apologize the evening after. His hair was wet as if he had just showered, and his usual sharp lines were hidden by orange flowing robes more like Tzeldea and the other doctors' clothes than his previous camouflage shirt and cargo pants. His anger had dimmed, but not withered completely, so he made a point to not acknowledge Huras until he had made three separate attempts to catch his attention.

Hey, k—whatever you want to be called right now. I know you can hear me.

He flinched minutely when Artist's expected snarky commentary didn't come. Resolutely, he lowered his right leg and continued the physical therapy exercises he'd managed to scrounge up from the depths of his memory. So far it hadn't been as difficult as he had feared, and he was still undecided whether that was because less time had passed than he'd thought or whether Dawi's time stasis technology had somehow been applied to counter his muscle atrophy. Scholar and Quartermaster would have been in a frenzy trying to figure out how many different useful applications selective time stasis could have outside of space travel.

You— Huras swallowed his insult with an audible gulp. I get it. You died and I suck. But we've got to work together here despite our personal feelings. Out of the corner of his eye, he saw Huras twist his hands awkwardly in the orange robes until he settled on folding his arms. They're suspicious of me, but you're just a victim. You can get far more information out of them than I can.

"A victim. That's what he thinks I'm useful as?" The void stared back, and he deliberately raised his left leg to the prescribed angle and took a deep breath. He all had always been too well known to do any sort of undercover work. He might've been the part who interacted with others the most, but acting was not something he had ever learned or wanted to do. A victim as an information pump. Not happening.

Blood runs thicker than water, he said when he had wrestled all his vitriol inside the mindhome and into the void. It will be a long time before I could force myself to like you.

That's fair, Huras said.

He lowered his leg and started on the next set of exercises. The sheets crinkled under him and the faint buzz of active machinery emanated from somewhere inside the walls. The quiet grated on the silence of the mindhome; the only times he had experienced this before was when most of the rest of him had been asleep.

Huras coughed and shuffled awkwardly, tapping his foot in that specific way the Ebicn drivers he met in information hubs and busy spaceports did. He noted that for later blackmail. When it became obvious he'd make no move to continue the conversation, Huras cleared his throat. So, are we going to start planning?

You'll remember I have next to no information except that which you've given me, he said dryly, or at least he thought that's what his tone indicated. It was certainly what his emotions broadcasted in the mindhome. Working together still left a bitter sponge in his stomach.

You clearly got to read more of the cndrid information than I did, since I had to obscure my base and got held up by the rest of— Huras gestured sharply, mouth quirking downward. You know. So what did you learn about this "blink" technology?

A growl rumbled through the mindhome, but never reached his throat. Part of him desperately wanted to strangle the engineer and make Huras say his name and roles, commit his victims to memory, but the rest of him was savagely glad Huras was unsure enough to avoid speaking on the subject directly. In the end he resorted to tugging his hair and forcing himself to sift through those last few memories where he had been whole, squinting past the pulsing ragged edges of the mindhome.

There wasn't much, he said eventually. I read most of a script for determining the bounds and targets of a localized dimension decoupling before you interrupted. It used the ancient mathematical notation, except the independent variable was time and not space. The process and the functionality wasn't something I read, or I suspect that you deciphered.

Huras responded with a barely concealed sneer. Well yes, I couldn't possibly have finished decrypting the code no one's been able to decipher before you Hirizcn lackeys got word and wanted to see the technology for yourself. Information travels fast, after all.

"Argh! We'll never get anywhere if we don't stop antagonizing each other," he hissed into the mindhome, crossing his mental arms and starting to pace. He needed Artist or Leader to pitch in, pull him out of his anger, and focus back on the mission to return home, but a step too far and he'd fall into the void again and effectively end the conversation. "What should I say?"

He'd probably have just ignored Huras's insult completely and continued on strictly business terms. Right. He let out a controlled exhale, sat up to face Huras properly, and tried to emulate Quartermaster's thought processes. Since other ruins similar to those on GU-T64A seemed to run on an unusually long-lived power source, it's likely that the cndrid's power core did the same, or else it was self-renewable.

Looking at Huras's odd orange clothes under the diffuse lights twigged another idea. What does Dawi's technology run on? Is it similar to what they used on GU-T64A?

Huras's shoulders actually relaxed and he finally flopped into a seat with a groan rather than towering over him. I wish. The natives stonewall me whenever I try to ask about their technology and every scan I can run discreetly returns with 'Unknown'. I got a peek at someone doing repairs on a wall light and it looks like they're not using the liquid in the cndrid core, though. Hotwiring a spaceship is decidedly out of the question.

That implied the civilization had moved to Dawi long enough ago that they had switched to a different form of energy. Was it because they'd been using a planet-specific resource, they'd moved to using a more convenient resource, or that their technology had just improved? He increased the pace of his steps in the mindhome, pleased with the logistical groove he was getting into.

"What kind of fuel were they using, then? Was it electrical? Geothermal? Planet-powered? Plasma-powered? Gamma or infrared, perhaps? No, that would have shown up on the scans. What did it look like? Was it on the visible spectrum? Was it a recognizable material? More description would be helpful, Huras.

"Is it possible they are using a heretofore unknown power source? Considering they invented time stasis without us knowing, I think it is a reasonable conclusion. Huras, I would like a reply soon." He looked up to glare and realized his mouth was not moving with the pace of his thoughts. His embarrassment broadcasted in the mindhome and he made a point of verbally clearing his throat. Ahem. What did the repair power source look like, then? We can extrapolate from there.

Huras wrinkled his nose in a way that made jealousy on his own behalf spike—what right did he have to wrinkle his nose like he all had?—staring into the middle distance as if he could synesthetically see his own calculations. It was likely some form of plasma or electricity, he said thoughtfully. I'm almost positive that was the power carrying medium and not the source, though. It's much easier to wire systems from one generator in urbanized planets.

So nothing like a ship's construction, then. Planetary architecture wasn't something he as Speaker had specialized in. He reached for the planet-specific power flow knowledge and grasped nothing. The void lashed out and caught the still-tender edges of his mind and tore, sending him reeling backwards both mentally and physically.

He blinked up at the ceiling. Colorful hand-painted geometric patterns stared back at him, faded blue and sienna intertwining over cream. Someone startled and sent a chair scraping backwards. The engineer bent over him, hair wet like he had just showered and dressed in robes like the doctors' and not his usual clothes.

Blast, kid—whatever you're called—are you okay?

When did you get here? he asked, cataloguing the muscle strain in his legs and the ache in his head. A glance in the mindhome showed blood in zero-g and he quickly focused outward. Did I just finish a procedure?

He got a premier streamer's view to seeing the freelancer's green eyes widen and his face fade to the shade of the ceiling above him. I'm— I'm going to get the doctors. The man stumbled back and left the room before he could formulate a reply, leaving him levering himself up and opening his mouth to an already closing door.

Chapter 6

Strange. He closed his eyes and brought his knees up so he could rest his head on them, trying to think without looking at the mindhome. Something was wrong. Besides the obvious, of course, but now was not the time to stare into the red-spotted darkness of the void. Had he fallen in again? But that would not explain the freelancer's reaction.

No, no, he should know the man's name. He introduced himself a while ago. H…Haris? Hubris? Hu…ras? Yes, that sounded right.

He opened his eyes again and stared at the blue cloth between his legs. Short term memory loss, then. His stomach flipped, twisted, and settled in the wrong position, like when Quartermaster had lost the correct position of a wiggly tooth when he had been young. The sensation had sent shudders up and down his all spines and had been disturbing enough that none of him could study until the tooth had been pulled out.

How much had he lost? Had this been common previously in his recovery, and he had just not had a marker of time to notice it? Was this going to be a permanent condition of his? What had triggered it? Was he going to have to live constantly assisted in case he had an episode, like the incurable form of epilepsy? Was he going to lose more and more pieces of himself until he was a vegetable, or until he became unconscious strands dissipating into the void? His breathing sped up and blood danced in his mental vision, tolling a death knell no matter how much he blinked.

The door hissed open and his head snapped up to see the psychologist hurry in with the man—Huras—hot on her heels. She took one look at him and firmly pushed his shoulders back, uncurling him to a proper sitting position so she could get a better angle to touch his head. Contrary to her brisk motions, she spoke a deliberate sentence that Huras scrambled to quickly translate.

We had been hoping this side effect would not happen, Huras read off of his padscreen. But it is a fairly common symptom of separation from a hivemind. Currently nameless one, you must think of yourself as an individual and not a collective. Until you are ready for healing, your soul cannot handle reaching out to others. He broke off and shook his padscreen at the psychologist, voice pitching and cracking oddly. What's that supposed to mean?

He spoke over Huras, urgency overriding the long-drilled importance of etiquette. This did qualify as a medical emergency. Is it permanent? Is it constant? Is there a way I can regain any lost memories? What do you mean, 'think of yourself as an individual'? Do you mean not to reach into the void? Why are you talking about a soul? Huras, stop ranting at her and translate me! It's far more important than venting your petty frustrations.

Petty? Do you want me to be happy your brain is a melted frying pan? Huras snapped to him, taking half a step forward before Tzeldea—oh, that was her name—shot a glare and he forcibly took a calming breath. He lowered his brows and glowered as he lifted his padscreen to his mouth, beginning to mutter the questions into the microphone. He guessed the engineer had improved his improvised translation program in the however long space of time he had lost.

The delay burned between his teeth as he tried to keep his shoulders relaxed and his head tilted in whatever direction Tzeldea wanted. There was no scanner she was using that he could see, but who knew what other wonders the time stasis using civilization would come up with. Scholar and Quartermaster would have loved to exchange information with them. The technological and cultural divide made it hard to effectively cooperate with her examination, though.

Finally, Huras's padscreen played the English translation and Tzeldea paused to shoot back an answer. Her deliberately calm tones did nothing but aggravate his frayed nerves. Right now he didn't dare turn inward to the mindhome, full of nothing but blood and the void rather than himself, and with no outlet he was vibrating with the strength of his emotions.

Huras scowled at the padscreen and read the translation, still sticking to accurate wording rather than the summaries he'd done previously that had been laced with sarcastic commentary. You are not ready for further treatment. Until then, it is possible that you may keep losing pieces of your short term memory. As long as you do not 'reach into the void', your mind should remain intact as the damage has already been done. Try not to reach beyond the borders of yourself as it is now. For now, that may be your working definition of thinking individually.

And the thing about the soul? he pressed. She was supposed to be a psychologist, wasn't she? But maybe that's what the soul terminology meant in this civilization.

Tzeldea took his chin and looked deep into his eyes so he couldn't track the progress Huras was making on the padscreen. He distantly noted they were the brown of cassia bark between the effort of trying not to either shrink away from her uncomfortably close face or look too deeply into his section of the mindhome. The blood there was settling, but it would be too easy to reach out if he was not focused on the outer world.

The translation played and Tzeldea looked at him for a few moments longer before drawing back and assuming a serious but thoughtful expression. Her words carried the cadence of a legend long learned, or a saying that had achieved ritual cultural status. They hit heavy and final in his ears, even though he was still waiting for the translation.

When we were separated, your civilization did not believe in the things not seen in this world. The soul lives and operates in another dimension, one not described easily by math, if you accept my analogy. Just as there are injuries of body and of the mind, there are injuries of the soul, and yours is one of them.

How do you know this? Huras growled into the padscreen before he could integrate Tzeldea's new concepts and information. He started to protest, but subsided when Huras added crossly to him, Oh don't bother. It's something we should know. Else how can we trust their sources?

For whatever reason, the question made Tzeldea hesitate and chew over her already slow-spoken words. He kept glancing between Huras and her and back again, unsure whose body language he should watch to gain the context clues he couldn't get from mutual understanding in the mindhome. His headache and heartache flared and he put a hand to his temple, slitting his eyes but still remaining outwardly present. There was no way he'd be able to maintain this state long term. How did anyone do it?

Finally, Tzeldea spoke and Huras stumbled through the unfamiliar terminology artifacts scattered through the translation. Demaniwel teaches us, both now and long ago. During the years your leaders have buried, many zoldiwe were made in a vrisgoth's image. We received many leaders, deserters, and survivors and learned to separate and heal many wounds of the soul. Is the art lost in all corners of your civilization? Ah, but as an escapee and a zoldiwe you two would not know.

His mental gears whirred, some spinning uselessly without the input of the rest of him but others drawing conclusions with astonishing speed. Demaniwel was some sort of well-known cultural figure, likely immortalized in media, someone who caused their initial split from the Agatian Concord over ideological differences. If he had access to the network, he could probably pinpoint the era and even the Gatik or English name of Demaniwel. No matter, that was something to assign to Scholar— No, Scholar was dead and he could not reach out without risking his memory. Wetness surprised him and he hastily moved his hands to wipe his face.

Back to the main thought process. Zoldiwe and vrisgoth? The first seemed to be a derivative of English "soldier", but he was nowhere near enough of a linguist to know if that was a viable assumption. But "deserters" did imply warfare, right? What kinds of wars would cause wounds of the soul? There were clear implications he was missing, he knew it, but without the clarification of a shared mindhome it was flying over his head. What important thing was he unable to grasp?

A flick to his nose startled his eyes open—he had closed them?—to find Tzeldea in his face again. She said something low and amused with a quiet smirk and offered a hand as if to pull him to his feet. Huras snorted, and when he looked at him for the translation, he said, She says to get out of your head, little one. See? I'm not the only one who thinks you're a kid.

That's in no way relevant to the current conversation. He internally winced at the warble that made it into his tone. Ask her what a zoldiwe is, and which of us she thinks the escapee is. And why does she want to wake me up?

Huras gave him an odd look. Wake you up?

He squinted and started to rub his temples as his productive thoughts began to slip through his fingers. Yes, that's what I said, isn't it? I always used to... Words failed him and he pushed away Tzeldea's hand so he could lean over and press his palms into his eyes.

Tzeldea's voice came firm and just barely sharp overhead, and a hand grabbed his forearm and pulled, hard. You're thinking too much, Huras read as Tzeldea tugged him off the bed and onto his feet. His legs stuttered and threatened to buckle, but Tzeldea slung his arm over her shoulder and had him marching toward the ornamented zigzag surrounding the door. I see your mind is one that must be occupied. Come, it is high past time you left this room. We will go to the Eating Garden. Perhaps then your healing can begin.

W— What? he muttered pitifully as the door hissed open and he tried to catch up with the situation. Tzeldea wrapped a steadying arm around his torso as he struggled to gain his footing, but she started down the right side of the hall as soon as he had found his center of gravity.

Looks like you're getting a field trip, kid, Huras laughed somewhere behind him. Doctor's orders.

CHAPTER 7

He smelled the garden before he saw it.

Every planet had its own distinct combination of scents; Artist and Quartermaster actually preferred to categorize his missions by scent for fast retrieval in the mindhome. Odor told him a lot about the relative safety and composition of a biome and its relative humidity, and it gave him a headstart on hesitantly categorizing the bioflora and fauna. His room had seemed odorless since he had long since gone noseblind, but the farther Tzeldea dragged him down the hallway the more he smelled sharp spices, fruity fragrance, and fresh, fertilized soil.

Are we going outside? he asked hesitantly, still holding his free hand to the side of his head.

What do you think? Huras drawled from somewhere behind, boots echoing off the walls and battering against his thoughts. Didn't the Eating Garden part tip you off?

He didn't dignify that with an answer. Frustration was bubbling behind his teeth and he didn't want to distract himself by starting another argument right as he went outside for the first time. Surprisingly, Tzeldea took hardly any turns, though the floor changed from smooth manufactured material to ceramic tiles to irregularly shaped cobblestones cheerfully echoing the geometric lines on the ceiling. Somewhere along the line the primary colors in the design had changed to yellow and green as well.

At last he found the cadence to Tzeldea's pace and began to match, pulling himself away from her support to walk under mostly his own power. She took a left and nodded swiftly to another orange-clad native in passing. He hastily gathered himself and attempted to smile, but by then the native was already long gone and the glow of natural light beckoned in the entrance ahead of them.

All the sensory input hit him with a narrow but potent blast, at once far less than he expected and overwhelmingly complex. Approximately half his mental resources were still occupied with not reaching out into the mindhome and he wasn't equipped to process all this data alone. It felt wrong to have to take the room in from only one perspective, integrating every impression all at once.

A large plexiglass biodome opened above them, latticed with golden metal supports that seemed to have the light, water, and atmospheric controls built into them. The air was humid, but not suffocatingly so, and chatter from all directions mingled with the sound of rushing water. People in colorful yet unsaturated robes were everywhere, with the majority wearing bangles, sashes, or other accessories with the geometric patterns that seemed to be cultural here. Most were in orange, green, or blue, with the blue ones almost always with one in orange or sitting in small clumps around stone tables. The pattern niggled at his mind, but not strongly enough for him to formulate any distinct hypotheses.

Trees, bushes, flowering plants, and vines were cut into clear sections with the cobblestone paths. Their groupings seemed purposeful, but with parasitic ferns hanging off fruit trees he wasn't sure whether it was meant to be aesthetic or practical. A tall plant similar to the chlorophyll spike he'd seen on GU-T64A caught his eye, and he started that way before he remembered he had no analysis equipment on him. He stumbled and Tzeldea caught his arm again, saying something in a mock scolding tone and steering him to a table that did not have anyone already sitting at it.

Do you like the scenery? Huras flopped down on a seat and leaned his elbows on the table, mouth twitching down when his sleeves got caught on the stone.

The floral scent was so much stronger at his seat, and he craned his neck to look at the tree hanging over them. Bulbous pink fruit hung from the branches, small buds poking through their glistening skin. It vaguely reminded him of the blue citrus Scholar had been itching to study at the beginning of this wretched mission. He blinked hard and jerked his mind away, wrestling down the ache welling towards his eyes and nose.

Hey, kid! I asked you a question.

He startled and turned his gaze to Huras just as Tzeldea flicked him, getting his ear instead of nose. "What?" They stared off for several seconds. Tzeldea sighed and said something to Huras that made him frown at his padscreen and mutter No into the microphone. He furrowed his brow, deciding whether to ask why Huras had asked him a question and promptly excluded him from the conversation. Part of his brain still tugged at the unintelligible conversations in the distance, interjecting distracting translation speculations into his productive thoughts.

Fine, have it your way. Huras tapped his padscreen violently, set it down with a thump, and stood, scowling. Whatever-you're-called, I'm going to fetch some lunch for us. The doctor's giving you your first therapy session. I've loaded my AI speech-to-text auto-translate alpha program and set it running. Don't you dare touch my padscreen. Huras glared harder for emphasis and walked away, periodically abruptly turning as if expecting him to grab the padscreen the moment his back was turned. It looked mildly ridiculous.

Tzeldea hummed and spoke in the measured tone that he was beginning to wonder was for easing translation. The delay as the program ran was significantly longer than Huras's live translations and he drummed a hand on the table to try to maintain his focus. At last an automated voice read, How are you feeling? Better than in the room?

Briefly, he considered downplaying his headache, but he brushed company protocol aside as soon as he realized most of him would have argued to take advantage of the only medical advice he had available. He took a moment to consciously block out the buzzing of some insect behind him and gather his thoughts into a concise verbal form. My head still hurts badly, but it's easier to remain focused on the outside world. More precisely, there was so much sensory input that he was too busy processing to have any internal thoughts to spare.

Tzeldea watched him shrewdly as the padscreen ran through the translation and played the reply. Good, she said back, tracing idle patterns on the tabletop. Please recount to me what you experienced of your memories.

What? Oh, she wanted to determine the extent of his memory loss. He mentally shrunk inward at the thought, but he had already decided to be forthcoming with her. Still, he remained on a laser's edge as he reached back through his memories, half expecting to find nothing at any moment and fall into the void.

It seems I lost a mix of explicit and episodic memory, including the latter parts of yesterday and most of today. I know Huras infuriated me and was sent away, and that we reconciled and had a conversation today, but I am not sure what. I did not remember either of your names at first. He wrinkled his nose, mentally gesturing at Scholar to make a note— No, he'd just have to remember to follow up with Huras himself.

Water dripped from somewhere above and splashed on his sleeve, but rolled off seemingly without issue. He alternated watching the drop's path and cataloguing Tzeldea's nonverbal tics while waiting for the translation and reply. Her face and shoulders stayed placid, leaving him unsure whether he was projecting his own frustration at the delays imposed on their conversation.

That is good. Remain tight within yourself and you will not suffer any more memory episodes. Tzeldea straightened, seemingly changing gears and speaking briskly, pausing to make gestures that underscored whatever point she was making. His headache spiked as he tried to log all her pictures so he could attempt to match them when the translation finally came through.

You are zoldiwe. Your soul is mixed so that you may share minds and hearts with one another. Now that you have been stripped away, you cannot hear them and your soul bleeds into the darkness. That was probably the hand swirling in the air. It is like a tapestry of many threads whose colors bleed together; you are a scrap who carries yellow, orange, green, and red as well as your natural blue. Tzeldea interlaced her fingers and made a slashing motion. The mental image was vivid and he winced.

Over time the bleeding will fade as wounds harden into scars. If you remain within the borders of yourself you will achieve this quickly, and the danger of further relapses will fade from the heart.

He waited a moment, but the translation seemed finished. Frowning, he rested his chin on his fist as he tried to process. A loud thump came from somewhere to the left and he startled, momentarily tensing for a confrontation before realizing it was someone dropping a basket of something. He simply didn't have enough attention to remain focused and stay aware of his surroundings.

With an internal growl, he blocked out the noise returned to the conversation. Fade from the heart? That was probably an odd cultural phrasing or a quirk of the auto translation program. Tzeldea had mentioned not being ready for further treatment before. Was this what she was referring to?

An idea came to him. He looked away from the void and made eye contact as he wet his lips. Is it possible to... his tongue balked and he shamefully stumbled, to 'mix' my soul with others? To have a hivemind again? After all, even as Bcqu it had taken several years before he had achieved full synchrony and learned to effectively communicate in the mindhome. Once the soul bleeding had scabbed over, wasn't it possible to simply start the mixing process once more?

No. As soon as the question finished translating, Tzeldea flicked her hand sideways. Your soul is too small to be mixed now. Zoldiwe cannot reform once broken, even with their original parts. Even if it were possible, we do not mix souls.

The hope that had hardly unfurled in his mind was crushed into so much perfume. The scent lingered pungent and sour on his tongue. The mindhome would forever remain a cold, ravenous, barely restrained void. His emotional connections and shared understanding would never be found again. Everything would always be swallowed up in suffocating silence and the holes in his memory.

Some of it must have shown in his expression, for Tzeldea's demeanour softened and she leaned forward, gentleness coloring her lowered tone. *Healing beyond scarring requires you to learn to live as an individual. It is hard, but there is no other way. Interaction with others may not come naturally to you, but you must have support to catch you when you stumble.*

Her intensity was too much for him and he drew away, shifting his gaze to the wide-leafed tropical fronds beyond her. Emotion fought its way out of the mindhome, leaking into his lungs and eyes. *Then I am doomed to a life of loneliness.*

Low metallophone music started playing, acting as some sort of signal. The ambient conversations shifted their flow as clumps broke up and began to drift away, out various doorways or into more organized groups of green, orange, and blue. Overhead, the sprinklers turned on and a fine, mineral-tinged mist started to come down.

Tzeldea's voice came earnest and soft, oozing with the false understanding that made him shudder. His breaths quickened and he clenched the table with both hands, not daring to close his eyes to try to ground himself. The padscreen's translation started playing, the salient information too distracting no matter how hard he tried to ignore it.

That is not true. There is another way.

Bitterness like the engineer's cynicism colored his words. And what would that be?

She spread her hands on the table and began tracing patterns once again, this time with the deliberate strokes of symbols well known. The padscreen's bland voice contrasted starkly against the nuance of Tzeldea's words. Demaniwel's way. We are separate, individuals, souls unique as the constellations of the stars, every planet and every soul beautiful in its own perspective. Yet we who are alive share Demaniwel's bond of connection. It is less clear and constantly intimate compared to your zoldiwe, but it is an unbreakable connection which transcends time and space.

"You don't understand. That's nothing like the selves I've lost!" he shouted into the mindhome, pacing a tight circle within the fragment he knew was safe. "You're saying I'm going to have to live forever like this. Forever watching myself, unable to form connections, incapable of relaxing for fear I fall back into the void! I can't keep living like this," he internally sank to his knees and clutched his chest, feeling the darkness crushing in on him.

"I can't survive long term like this," he repeated, and the emptiness swallowed it whole.

CHAPTER 8

Putting his physical face in his hands, he roughly brushed the tears from his eyes. The despair he had felt when he first began to regain consciousness grappled him, and without the rest of his support he had no motivation to fight against it. He knew what he said was true. Already one full day-cycle of awareness had cost him one major memory loss episode, and despite his attempts he had already had far too many close calls with reaching into the void. One day-cycle, sooner than later, he would forget himself and reach so deep the emptiness would consume him, and he would unravel just like the rest of himself had done.

Can't I just go home? he asked from the darkness in his hands. He still had a duty to return to Hirizcn and report his deaths, and they could at least attempt treatment before he would die himself. But no, if he was going to be leaving this planet he should at least bring Huras with him. If you lend Huras and I a ship we will leave you alone. I just want to die in peace.

Laughter pealed in the distance and fragrant mist beaded on his neck. His heart and mind hurt and all he wished for at the moment was to have Leader so he could pass on these burdensome decisions. The translation played in ancient English and Tzeldea made a wounded noise, sliding along the seats until an arm wrapped around his shoulders and gently squeezed.

I cannot, she said, voice laden with pain and regret. Once the door is open, your people will come conquering and we will not be able to close it. I am deeply sorry.

Why? More tears wet his hands and his voice twisted in the way that he had not heard outside the mindhome in a decade. The void of the mindhome stared back at him, indifferently swallowing his cries.

Once we almost lost our history and we do not forget again. Your people crossed dimensions and failed before, and when they failed they came to take from us. If we let you go back, even the distance of the stars we have put between us will not be enough to stop those tragedies from happening again, and we would not be the cause of forming more vrisgoth.

So this civilization must have left during the wars of Agradulan, when the precursor to Zilcn drives had been failing and the Partu powers had been looking for technological alternatives. The resulting resource conflicts had birthed the methods that had created him and the others of his kind. He looked sideways for Quartermaster's wave of triumphant realization and his heart wrenched when he saw only the void.

Despair warred with anger as he realized Tzeldea's words were right. If he went back to Hirizcn, his report or even the ship he arrived in would provide the Zilcn drive solution they had been discreetly searching for. To Tzeldea's people, sending him back would be tantamount to igniting another long series of wars.

We would not conquer you, he said feebly, bracing himself for another death to his flickering hope. Hirizcn prides itself on being a transparent company who upholds all standards of moral practice and implementation.

He felt rather than saw Tzeldea's hand flick sideways, her arm sliding down to rub the lower half of back. I cannot accept that to be true.

He jerked his head up to stare at her, long engrained pride flaring and hardening his shoulders into professional offense. She quickly pulled back and lifted up her hands, speaking quickly with smooth brows tilted downward. The delay as the padscreen processed was charged with lurid silence.

A mixed soul brings pain. I speak from the many records that the zoldiwe and vrisgoth who came to us left behind. That you are a zoldiwe broken when you come to us speaks ill of this company you seek to protect.

Emotions swirled in his mind, fighting for dominance and expression. With nowhere to go in the mindhome, disgust won out and curled his lip a little before he wrestled his face back under control. He turned his face from Tzeldea and stared pointedly at a fragrant, feathery-leafed bush. How did anyone function without support in the mindhome? All the years of socialization training told him he should listen and not dismiss foreign ideas out of hand, but with no Artist or Quartermaster or Scholar to delegate information processing while he tried to talk through his emotions, he could not keep an impartial expression. The tears that had no understanding answer kept pricking at his physical rather than mental eyes.

"A mixed soul brings pain. How could anyone who is like me say that? It's killing me off or 'breaking me' that brings pain. And it's not the company's fault I died, it's Huras's!" His shout died within half a second of making it and no response came from the void.

The padscreen crackled and made a jingle that likely signaled low battery. You do not have to accept this, it read out a little after. But wrong or not, you are separated now and you must learn to live as an individual.

He felt Tzeldea hesitantly move closer but did not acknowledge her, hands gripping the table again hard enough his knuckles turned white. No, he did not accept that his very existence was wrong and doomed to bring pain. He did not accept that her diagnosis meant he would never form an emotional connection again. He most certainly did not accept that the fault for his deaths fell on anyone except Huras. He had to find a way to release his anger without lashing out at someone outside the desolate mindhome.

Let me be, he grit out, vaguely astonished that of all things Artist's temper had managed to survive the tearing of his soul, but too furious to feel any satisfaction from discovering other surviving parts of himself. I do not want to hurt you.

A sigh, and a rustle as Tzeldea stood and moved a couple of steps away. He caught orange at the corner of his eye clambering onto the seat she'd just been on and reaching up to pick one of the fruit from the overhead branches. She sat down almost across from him and began to peel it, presence unobtrusive and gaze seemingly wholly focused on digging her thumbs through the thick pink rind.

Looked like that was the most privacy he would get. Closing his eyes and letting out a controlled breath, he fisted his hands and turned away. This anger was unproductive, he tried to tell himself. He had been the Speaker, he was better than this. He should wait until Tzeldea dumped him back in his hospital room, and then he could rage freely in relative privacy. She was attempting to be gentle with him, all things considered.

Then again, anger was better than depression and the despair that she would not even let him go back to Hirizcn, or the despair at his future continued existence. Those wretched self-care lectures that survived in his memory told him grief was slow and non-linear, and that bouncing between these emotions was progress, but right now he did not care. At least back at Hirizcn he could prosecute Huras for manslaughter and potentially murder.

A cold finger touched his back and he whipped around, reflexively drawing a machete that was no longer there. Tzeldea leaned across the table, arm outstretched with a crescent-shaped section of pale pink fruit, exterior removed. I can see that this is hard for you, she said softly. Will you allow me to help you?

He looked down at the fruit, adrenaline briefly pushing back his brambled mess of emotions. This was a moment of cultural or interpersonal significance, his intuition screamed it. But with his logical facilities out of commission, he had no idea what he should do. Did he even want to associate with Tzeldea beyond the bare necessity?

Scholar-like, he flipped through the information that came to attention without reaching into the potential blanks in his memory. Refusing a gift was almost universally rude, refusing a gift of food even more so. But accepting a gift often implied a debt or promise of future obligation, and the methods for gracefully refusing a gift were culture-specific and the details eluded him. Right now the obvious meaning was a symbolic acceptance of this civilization's help. Subtextually? He was supposed to be the expert, but with so little information and so much sensory interference everything except intuition continued to escape him.

A dewdrop fell from his nose in a twisted mockery of the frustrating tears he could not seem to keep inside. The fruit glimmered, plump with untapped possibility. He shook his head violently and tried to push away his intrusive thoughts, but Tzeldea's expression and offer remained the same.

Anger and despair mixed into the sordid taste of bitterness, and his shoulders hunched at the cynical thought that came to him. "What does it matter anyway?" It wasn't like really, in the end, he had any other choice. As a medical professional, Tzeldea could and would provide emergency medical care until the day-cycle he could not be recovered any more, and with him and the murderer stuck on Dawi, Tzeldea's civilization held all the power and all the cards.

Dully, he took the pink section and ate it, resentfully savoring the citrus-like explosion of sweet and sour in his mouth. Fine, he said when he had chewed and swallowed, the foreign taste lingering in a tingle in his throat. What other choice do I have?

CHAPTER 9

Huras returned with three packages of steaming long-grained rais and vegetables, a dripping wet front, and a thunderous scowl. When pressed, he said that he got lost looking for a bathroom, and when he found one, the tap fixtures did not agree with him. Tzeldea seemed torn between stifling amusement and showing sympathy, but he hunched his shoulders and shoveled down his food as quickly as possible, chewing just enough to swallow without choking.

There were spices he didn't recognize, something like turmeric and cardamom and garam masala, and he was halfway through constructing a flavor profile to submit to Quartermaster before he realized that he was the lone survivor and could not play the guess-the-flavor game with himself any longer. The thought reminded him in turn about his conflicting texture preferences, and all motivation to finish his food vanished. Swallowing, he harshly reminded himself that adequate nutritional intake was necessary and forcefully turned his attention away from tear-fraught memories.

With translation once again restricted through Huras, Tzeldea didn't try to continue conversation for long. He suspected she was giving him space to process, like she had the first time. It was probably part of this civilization's medical training for soul healing or whatever. 'A mixed soul brings pain' and all that. He consciously stopped, screamed long and loud in the mindhome, and resumed mental pacing on a slightly less cynical train of thought. What were the viable ways of expressing emotion when there was no one in the mindhome? Did he dare search through his memories for information on individuals' emotional coping mechanisms? The constant meaningless chatter of distant conversations stabbed his ears and exacerbated his headache that still hadn't gone away.

Huras clapped his hands and startled him out of his thoughts, nearly causing him to choke on his final mouthful. Well, we've eaten now. I'm sure Tzeldea has other things to do, so I'll take you back to your room. Come on, you can help me put these containers away.

Frustration won out over discretion and he scowled at the engineer with all of his—no, just his now—face. No. I need some time alone. Time alone to face his problems, time alone to destroy something harmless, time alone to once more convince himself not to fall into the void. Time to process his emotions and persuade himself that Tzeldea's offer was more than a condescending power play that would condemn him to a life of prolonged suffering.

Don't be stupid. It won't take long. Huras wiggled his eyebrows and stressed the word.

He snapped his teeth shut on the flash of insight and following groan that threatened to escape into the physical world. "Wet because bathroom taps didn't agree with you indeed," he hissed vitriol into the void of the mindhome. "Why do you have to drag me into this?"

I can escort myself, he bit out. My muscles aren't that atrophied.

Now he was looking, Huras's demeanour was so blatantly casual it raised Lead— his flags. For all his difficulty with understanding others' motivations it was clear the engineer had been poking around where he shouldn't have been. He refrained from pointing out the hopelessness of figuring out a foreign civilization's revolutionary technology when Tzeldea's people were more than aware of the danger Huras's escape would cause. Surely Tzeldea had already crushed his hopes as well, and he was just being stubborn.

Tzeldea touched Huras's arm and said something short with a hint of platinum, but he shrugged it off and wiggled his eyebrows again with another significant look. Better over than undercompensated.

If Artist were alive, he would be using the table he habitually made in his part of the mindhome as a surface to repeatedly bang his head against. Short of directly antagonizing him, was there anything he could say to get Huras to leave him out of his schemes? He wanted to go back to his room and block out the world for a while. Communication with others was supposed to be his specialty, but all he could think of was to acquiesce and get it over with.

Well then. If he blew up, it would be the murderer's own fault. Fine.

Huras briefly argued with Tzeldea before coming over and bending down so he could sling an arm over his wet shoulders. Pointedly, he used the table to push himself up and stood on his own. The engineer still put a hairy arm around to support him and started speedwalking deeper into the garden, hissing as soon as the various flora blocked Tzeldea entirely and thoroughly from sight. What's gotten into you? Did you forget our agreement?

What agreement? he blurted reflexively, climbing vines, foreign voices, and a startling sense of deja vu distracting him from a frantic search through the patches of his most recent memories. Huras had to be referring to one of the conversations he lost.

Refuse-soaked drive clutches, we don't have time for this. The hitch in Huras's step belied the heat in his tone. You're helping me find a way to escape. Our current theory is that this civilization is powered from centralized sources that may or may not use a separate power carrying medium. I've been exploring whenever I can and investigating whether their power source is the same as the one in the cndrid I found.

Rounding a corner, Huras narrowly dodged walking them both into a clump of green-clad natives. His teeth clacked together painfully as Huras jerked them against some overly earthy bushes to let the others pass, and he swallowed his growl to let his free hand block out some of the increasingly overwhelming stimulation. You are coming to give me your professional opinion on whether the electricity in these buildings is being used as the source or as a carrying medium.

It's hopeless. The words escaped him, and he was horrified at how easy it was becoming to verbalize his directed thoughts rather than voice them in the mindhome. Reverse engineering this will take years, and if they're smart Tzeldea's people will never let us close to their intersystem ships. Even then, it'd take precious hours to plot our course to a viable star system.

Huras's head whipped around to stare at him before firming his mouth into a grim line and speeding up his steps even more. They swirled around several corners in quick succession, containers rattling and colors swirling enough that he closed his eyes and hung his head so he could only focus on the mist beading on his hair and running down his face.

The air dried and darkened as they passed from the garden into an undefined hall. Huras's distinctive boot clomping became far more noticeable as the floor changed back to tiles and smooth material once again. He counted five minutes of gradually more oppressive silence before Huras suddenly knocked his feet out from under him and dumped him on a woven chair. Eyes flying open, he reached for his nonexistent toolbelt and braced an arm defensively, but Huras just shoved him back and brandished the empty containers in his face.

Life is different than your sheltered little fetch quest missions, he growled with such force he almost felt physically struck. You don't just wait around and get your life's goals handed to you on a silver platter. Get it into your head, he punctuated each syllable with a finger jabbing at his face, this is NOT Hirizcn. Stop believing everything they say. If they don't want us to go back, we just have to go and take it ourselves.

His nose flared, offended, but he hardly opened his mouth before Huras cut him off.

It is NOT hopeless! The only reason I can ever get anything outside of your bloodsucking corporations is because I go out and try. This situation is no different. You might be willing to give up and die ten thousand lightyears away from home, but I am not. I, unlike you, have someone to get back to. Whirling, Huras sat himself in a chair opposite, crossing his arms and huffing through tightly clenched teeth.

Different responses flew through his mind too fast to even verbalize in the mindhome: "You're not the one recovering from a life-changing injury," "You still haven't answered my points about logistics," "Hope doesn't change cold, hard reality," "What do I care if you have someone to go back to?", all twisting around each other and causing only a strangled sound to emerge from his throat. His hands found the lengthening spikes of his hair and squeezed, desperately trying to reestablish some semblance of grounding and emotional control in this situation.

He was stretched too thin for this. Between Tzeldea's revelations and the emotional fallout, the overstimulation of attempting to process a complex world on his own, and the post-memory loss headache that still throbbed behind his temples, he just had no energy to try to parse out another conversation. Curling up on the woven chair, he ignored the sitting-room-equivalent and Huras glowering across from him and did his best to completely retreat into his mind.

He stared at blood turned purple and jagged pieces scattered beneath his feet, crashing emotions howling like that one planet's hurricane winds now that there was no true mindhome to share his connections with. Leader and Scholar particularly had grounded him, pinned his roiling feelings into strong, flowing currents whenever one of him began to spiral out of control. Now that their corners were ripped and thrown into the darkness those currents flailed like olden tent stakes ripped free and flapping in the gale.

He had no idea what to do. He barely kept track of his own thoughts as his internal metaphors strengthened and became more distinct in the mindhome, emotion winds buffeting his clothes and shards of himself sharpening and cutting through his soles and into his feet. It was like Artist to get lost in the mindhome, blessed with the talent for mental manipulation but constantly caught up in internal projections rather than reality. He no longer had the memories of how to take control of the mindscape and calm himself down.

Stay within the bounds of himself. Find out whether electricity was truly the main power source with the goal of decoding 'blink' space travel. Process the concept of living his entire life alone. Redefine parameters and sense of self in view of his likely incoming morality. Sleep. Figure out a way to get rid of this performance-collapsing headache. Return to his room before Tzeldea came looking for him. Reorganize his thinking habits to handle processing external input by himself. Grieve.

His thoughts spun round and round, never lingering long enough to make progress toward answers. He heard Huras get up and walk out, presumably to return the containers and hopefully return to take him back to his room. Planning for the likelihood Huras didn't return joined the chaotic mix.

Untold time passed like when he had first begun regaining consciousness after the blink. Slowly, his thoughts and emotions blew themselves out like a storm and he mentally and physically slumped, exhausted. Evidently 'wait it out' was a valid strategy for inner conflict when all else failed. Without moving, he vaguely wondered if that information had used to be catalogued in Artist, Leader, or Scholar's lost expertise.

He lingered briefly before pulling his focus back toward the physical world and running over his most recent set of problems. First: finding Huras. As much as he loathed to admit it, he did not think he was capable of making it back to his room on his own strength and he hadn't noticed the route they had taken from the garden anyway. Short of Huras returning or throwing himself on some helpful native despite a language barrier, he was stuck.

Say if Huras returned. He would have to address the unresolved end of their conversation. He did still think that attempting to return to known space would be a long and grueling endeavor, but he had, evidently, made an agreement with Huras. His response had been out of line. He would have to apologize.

Huras chose that moment to come back in, no longer carrying the food containers and noticeably calmer. Something eased in his shoulders when he saw that he was cognizant again, but his lips still twitched downward. Huras paced behind the brown chair he had sat in earlier and folded his arms, letting the silence stretch as he scrambled to construct a sufficiently inoffensive apology.

Well? he said finally. Is your brain working again?

He sputtered on the beginnings of his explanation, coughed, and shook to clear his head with a wince. His brain hadn't stopped working, he'd chosen to block the outside world out. Had Huras been trying to talk to him and he'd been unresponsive? Was that not something non-hiveminded individuals did occasionally?

Focus. Yes, he got out, trying to keep his voice neutral. Today has been rather...overwhelming. I spoke emotionally earlier. I apologize for my catastrophizing behavior. That certainly came out too formally, but he could not remember the appropriate formulae. Just move the conversation on. So, what did you want me to look at?

Huras rolled his eyes, but uncrossed his arms to take out his padscreen. Thank you for waiting for me to accept your rusty apology. I'm sure the feeling is mutual. Turning his screen to show an incomplete map, he pointed at the blinking cursor in a room off one of the larger hallways. This is the repair bay I found on the way back from the kitchens. Two hours ago a ship's innards were open and I got a decent look at the workings. You're coming over and confirming if electricity is the main power source or the carrying medium. Failing that, I'll bring you to a bathroom and we'll look at the building's light system instead.

He closed his eyes, briefly gauging his energy reserves. He probably should manage. Fine. I don't think I can go too long, though. I'm fighting a grade three point five headache. He gingerly pressed a palm on his temple, fighting a sour grimace.

A brief expression flashed across Huras's face, but he tucked his padscreen back into his robes and walked around the chairs without further comment. Come on, he said, bracing and offering an arm. Up you get.

Chapter 10

Now that he wasn't fighting shutdown, walking in the hallways wasn't bad at all. At this point he strongly suspected the geometric patterns on the floor and ceiling were culturally specific and functional, as groups of strings would break off the prevailing tangle and begin a new pattern at every branching corridor. Huras hadn't seemed to notice and was following the map on his padscreen rather than the pale yellow strands on the ceiling.

They drew a lot of eyes walking down the corridor, but no one stopped them and Huras was not bothered even when he warily brought the subject up. I'm one of your assigned caretakers and you're an inpatient. He waved his padscreen at Huras's own orange robes and his contrasting blue hospital gown. Unless they know about your situation specifically they're going to assume I know what I'm doing. Which, I do.

"That seems like a rather faulty security system for inpatients," he muttered. They passed through a foyer with various potted fronds and a domed plexiglass ceiling like the Eating Garden's and took a hard right, still following the pale yellow lines. "All I'd have to do to compromise the system is steal some clothes and look like I belong."

Huras made no answer and continued in focused silence as they began to make several turns along increasingly peripheral passageways. He consciously stopped himself from reaching for Scholar's opinion on the cultural color coding of the patterns, realized he had spoken in the mindhome rather than in the external world, and again pushed himself through the distraction of his headache to reassess his state. Oh. His legs were beginning to shake from all the exercise and Huras was having to take more and more of his weight.

Sharp, fruit-tinged acidic scents blasted them as they passed through a restraining firsficld into a large, open bay, mixing with the more familiar odors of lubricant and heated metal. Strong, humid winds buffeted workers wrapped in yellow clothes more reminiscent of Palagian desert planets than Huras or Tzeldea's robes. Compact spheroid spacecraft and more typical aerodynamic aircraft were suspended in firsficlds scattered around the bay, all in various states of gutting and attended by at least two cndrids.

Huras hurried them around a deactivated shield generator and let him slide to the floor. He didn't protest, slightly dizzy from all the input and rather alarmed at how low his tolerance levels had become. Carefully scratching over his intact memories, he found a faded record of a grounding technique he had learned before the mindhome had been formed and ran through it, bringing his hands up around his knees and wringing his fingers while rocking back and forth. The motion felt like picking up a long forgotten squish toy, strange at first but easily returning to well-worn familiarity.

Huras watched him, first puzzled and then with realization, and by the time Huras spoke again he had stabilized and returned himself to acceptably functioning levels. Strangely, his posture and stance had dramatically softened and his mouth didn't curl with partially concealed disgust. Are you sure you can handle this? We can always come tomorrow. This is your first day-cycle outside your room.

Are you changing your mind now? he muttered back, grip tightening as he tried to determine the realization that had driven Huras's sudden change. He didn't like it when people changed their minds while they were talking to him. He hardly ever figured out the thinking driving their imperceptible motivations. Besides, even accounting for my current— injury, I am functional. Let's finish the mission and get it over with.

Huras frowned and took on a sterner posture. You shouldn't—

Do you want me to help you or not? You yourself said that a ship's interior is currently accessible. There's no guarantee of that tomorrow, he snapped, hoping his attack would anger Huras and return their relationship to comprehensible antagonism. He didn't have Leader or Scholar or Artist any more, and he heavily relied on his perspectives to make accurate judgments of other minds. Huras was making this entire mission harder than it needed to be.

Rather than sniping back, Huras thinned his mouth and stood to peek around the generator. Four repetitions of the grounding finger twists later, Huras retreated and crouched to pull him back into a supported standing position. The one at 130 lat is unoccupied for the moment. Not the same ship, but it looks intersystem worthy and it's out of sight line from the entrances. Quickly, on three.

Pushing past the unwanted reminder that he counted down every mission for the rest of himself, he braced his aching legs to sprint across the open area. Despite his efforts, Huras effectively dragged him the whole way. They slowed down just enough to duck under the generator through the firsficld entrance and slump on the floor, panting and beginning to sweat despite the constant wind. He used his comparatively fresh arm muscles to drag himself forward a few meters and flip over to get a good long look at the exposed workings. Most of the actual components he could match to his understanding of ships, but on a first pass the overarching structure of the network was inscrutable to him.

Lifting an arm, he pointed at the open panel where the Zilcn drive would usually be. I don't see the power core. The red wires seem to be routed to the door and rockets, but I don't know what that pipe is supposed to be. Surely the ventilation system shouldn't be entangled with the nonessential equipment? And where is the life support? He reached for a schematic he knew Scholar had memorized and hastily jerked away when he teetered on the void.

Huras grunted. That motherboard on the left is broken. The other one I looked at did not have such jagged edges. Whatever it is, it's important enough we're not seeing any power come through. That's unfortunately the downside of looking at broken ships. Does it ring any bells for your Hirizcn-trained mind?

He squinted and got onto his elbows to get a better look at the panel in question. It was sleek, painted black, and triangular with irregularly serrated edges. Tiny grooves crisscrossed its surface, glinting gold and reminding him of...

It's electrical, he said definitively. The etching is reminiscent of pre-quantum technology. I'll guess that the golden material is conductive while the black material is not, and the surrounding wiring does look electricity compatible. I have no idea what the shape would be for, though. He swallowed and looked away from Scholar's section of the void. "Not as I am now."

Robes rustled and Huras sat up, gently poking one or two pipes of dubious material and craning his neck to try get a better look at the machinery deeper inside. Yeah, figured as much. How did they generate enough electricity to power near-instantaneous space travel, though? It's not nearly reliable enough... He descended into muttering.

Instantaneous? He didn't remember any travel time, but he'd assumed that the shock of his deaths had rendered him unconscious or otherwise insensible for the whole duration. The cndrid code he'd read had said time stasis, though... What did it mean to decouple and manipulate the time dimension rather than space?

Yeah, that's why they call it a blink, Huras said without looking, taking pictures of the mechanics and making quick sketches on his padscreen. One moment we're crashing and the next I'm standing on a big open platform and you're keeling over. I haven't been able to find my ship anywhere since. He made a final slash and returned to muttering about electricity and dimensional couplers.

"Nowhere?" Thankfully, he kept his blurted question in the remains of the mindhome, as even he knew that separating a captain from his personal ship was an unacceptable social offense. Questioning Huras's commitment to locating his ship would only cause an argument and it sounded like Huras was falling into a deductive engineering flow.

Still, a ship and everything on it disappearing in an instant, transporting them an incredible distance by manipulating decoupled time rather than space... Those were some key conceptual clues to understanding this civilization's space travel, and from there discovering how to return home. Electrical power, a reversed equation, disappearing objects...did the cndrid that initiated the blink disappear with them as well?

He rolled over and sat up, poking Huras's leg to get his attention. When we appeared, was the cndrid with us?

No, Huras growled, Now let me focus—

Egadu miri bugin? a crisp, tightly modulated voice interrupted from behind them.

Chapter 11

Huras whirled, him scrambling to follow a half second later. A distinctly square cndrid rolled around the firsficld generator, hip height and made of polished yellowed metal. Unlike the original cndrid that had started all this, its carapace was hardly segmented and seemed both easily replaceable and well maintained. It spoke again, gesturing sharply and rolling back and forth as if pacing. The adrenaline of getting caught warred with his Artist-like curiosity of whether Dawi allowed looser restrictions on the relative believability of humanoid AI.

May my luck suffocate in negative dimensional space, Huras hissed while furiously tapping on his padscreen. I haven't got enough data to even start a working translation of Dawihcn yet. Two-way English to Gatik with a dictionary was hard enough.

What are we going to do? he said, internally screaming at having to ask the freelancer and desperately keeping himself from reaching for Leader's void. We're too identifiable to successfully run.

Either pretend we're idiots or play up you being depressed. Huras gestured shortly and shot a venomous glare at the cndrid.

Nausea coiled in his intestines. "Emotions aren't something you should manipulate for fun, or they will control you." He stared into Artist's part of the void and shook his mental head. "But as Quartermaster would say, it's not like I have many options here. I don't think I can do extra emotions without falling straight into depression again."

The cndrid spoke again, sharper, and raised an arm in a signal before beginning to roll away. Huras lunged and caught its elbow, dragging it back toward him. Think fast, kid. Being something other than a nonfunctional BSOD would be helpful about now!

He shook himself, redid the shake in the physical world, and scooted several steps back to help visualize turning away from the void. Their mission had been discovered. Objective: either escape without getting caught or bluff or lie out of any consequences. He wasn't good at acting, not even as he had been before, Huras was busy fighting a losing battle against the cndrid's strength, they couldn't talk it down or somehow verbally bypass its mental programming—!

No. Hold that thought. Can you hack into it? he asked, pitching his voice over the cndrid's increasingly terse proclamations. Use the program you used to decipher the original cndrid's blink. Wipe its memories of us or at least install a block on reporting us.

I'm— flattered you think that— I'm hirable enough— for that quick of an effective rush job, Huras panted, jerking the cndrid back one step and losing three. This— is at least— three generations— beyond that relic of spaghetti code. Ouch! Huras stumbled into the firsficld and jolted, losing his balance and landing hard on his tailbone. His padscreen clattered out of his sleeves.

The cndrid stopped rolling away and hovered, presumably buzzing a safety warning. Not a moment to lose. He scrambled for the padscreen, briefly glaring at Huras when he didn't get up before remembering that as another mind, Huras had no way to know his plans. He had to verbalize. Words, words, his attention was too focused on finding an analogue to a maintenance port on the cndrid, why was verbalizing so difficult under pressure?

There! Levering himself on the cndrid's yellow-plated arm, he jabbed a diamond shape in the engravings on the back of its neck, the only noticeable spot of negative space. The cndrid beeped plaintively before powering down and sliding a large portion of its back open, similar to the old Agatian models Scholar had studied for one of his Historic Technology certification learning modules.

Oh. He blinked down at Huras's padscreen, powered on but still behind its security vault. It was incredibly fortunate the memories he'd been unconsciously accessing had not been ones lost to the void. If he reverted to his usual habits like this any moment he was under time pressure, it was going to be near impossible to prevent himself from reaching and falling headfirst into the void. His hand shook and he hastily lowered himself to the floor, drawing his knees up so he could restart his grounding routine.

Huras stalked over and snatched the padscreen from his hands. Copyright thief! I told you not to touch my padscreen.

It's still locked, he said dully, looking at his knees, clasping his fingers together, and already turning his focus inward. The cndrid's there. Go hack it and get us out of here.

Huras's blue robes hesitated in his peripheral vision. Two deep breaths, and then a long sigh. Knee jerk reaction. Don't take it personally. With several unsavory mumbles, his boots clomped over to the cndrid and began picking over potential ways to adapt the inputs of the maintenance port. The thrum and high whine of the firsficld took over silence once more.

There was no feasible way to avoid stressful situations for the rest of his life. Even if he submitted himself wholly to Tzeldea's mysterious treatment plan, there was bound to be another moment where he and Huras were nearly caught in their subterfuge. And if he escaped... His remaining expertise lay nearly solely in time-sensitive, threatening situations. The likelihood of a short life loomed before him again, suffocating like his first few moments in the void.

This is going to take more than a few minutes. We should get out of here before someone comes to work on this ship. Huras straightened and gave the cndrid an experimental push. It didn't roll until he reached down and released some emergency brake. Huras grunted approvingly and stashed his padscreen, not meeting his eyes. Can you walk yourself?

"He wants to take the cndrid?" He forced himself not to flinch when nothing echoed back from the void. Every time he began to get remotely comfortable, he slipped up and reminded himself of his deaths again. "I suppose that makes sense." Realization struck him and zapped energy up his spine. "If we can hide the cndrid long term, we can hack it properly and learn Dawi's technology. It was in the repair bay, so it likely knows how to operate intersystem ships and initiate blink."

That only left logistics. He experimentally tensed his calves and winced. No, he admitted tersely. Definitely not fast enough to cross the open area without being seen. That raised problems for transporting both him and the cndrid. Glancing at the firsficld gap reminded him that the repair bay outside was also full of overwhelming scents and sounds, causing his headache to flare. He was definitely going to be a dead weight liability. Shame burned under his frustration at the entire situation.

Huras did not state the obvious, though he was fairly sure he saw annoyance on his face. Fine. You first, all the way into the hallway, then the cndrid. As Huras crouched down and arranged his grip on him, he caught a sour mutter. If not for my rusty hair, I could probably stroll in and out with the cndrid and no one would flag an anomaly.

He gritted his teeth as they stood, pain lancing across his calves and inner thighs as he started using those muscles again. Really, it would have been much easier if either of them had had similar builds or skin tones to the natives' melanin-rich, rounded features. What about getting a head wrapping like the workers over there? Or would that require a whole outfit change?

An outfit change, probably. Have you somehow missed this civilization's blatant color coding? Huras scoffed, shifting his arm more comfortably over his shoulders and pausing at the gap in the firsficld. Brace yourself. We step out on 3.

Closing his eyes, he inhaled deeply and mentally steadied himself. Focus on getting across the space quickly, without stumbling. Attempt to block out extraneous sensory input. He could do this, even if he was all alone.

They burst through the gap and into the whirlwind of acidic fruit and machinery and buffeting wind. He forced his legs forward as quickly as possible, breathing through his mouth to lessen the smells. They rounded the dormant firsficld generator, paused for seven precious seconds, and stumbled into the hall, the static of the firsficld and the sudden noise cutoff perforating his narrow focus and making his steps stutter. The more neutral scents of tile and cleaner was a relief that almost made up for the increasing pain of his headache.

Huras dumped him in the closest empty sitting room and hurried back for the cndrid, giving him a few moments to recenter himself. The headache was moving to behind his eyes. Ugh. At this rate, when he finally made it to his room to rest he was going to crash and sleep all the way through the remainder of the day-cycle. Huras would have to figure out how to deal with the cndrid himself. He was more than spent enough, especially for it being his first trip outside his room during recovery.

Recovery and rehabilitation, learning to live as a single body forever removed from the rest of himself. Learning how to escape or integrate into a foreign society and not to be incapacitated by a mildly busy room.

Learning, somehow, to walk in his own confidence without un-ravelling into the void.

No. He pressed his palms into his eyes and gently chewed his lip. He'd already had at least two major breakdowns today. He was not going to have a third. Life-changing (life-shortening) revelations or not, he would keep himself stable until this mission was over and he had had a good rest. He was still capable of that, at least, surely.

The telltale clunk of Huras's boots preceded his huffing entry into the room, pushing the deactivated cndrid in front of him. Without a word, he examined the room and rolled the cndrid by the table in the corner, proceeding to carefully position its open back out of view. There. The amount of kafii rooms there are in this place is ridiculous, but it's convenient. I think that should pass a casual inspection for at least half an hour. Prosperity-trusting idiots, the lot of them, even with the whole fuss about keeping secrets from us.

Strangely, his carefully calmed emotions flinched and caused a barely audible grumble in the mindhome. His experience so far had been woefully limited to Tzeldea and a couple of other doctors, of course, but so far his prevailing impression is that they were far kinder than most professionals, not overly trusting. Granted, their security was lacking, but from his conversation with Tzeldea and suspicions about their ideology he doubted it was due to blindly trusting prosperity.

Physical brow furrowing, he stopped and reexamined those last trains of thought. Was he being defensive of Tzeldea and her people? So far he had been fairly unimpressed by Tzeldea's approximation of mental health care and society, but if he was defensive of her... Another uncomfortable set of questions settled into his stomach.

He was operating far below acceptable levels at this point; both Quartermaster and Leader would have long since ordered him off the mission. He needed to end this overly taxing self-imposed mission and sleep. Drawing himself up, he lowered his hands and set his stance in an approximation of his "authoritative confidence" reference in his mental body language catalogue. If we have half an hour, I need to return to my room.

Huras pulled out his padscreen, checked the time, and hissed in a breath. You're right. Tzeldea will definitely be suspicious. I'll have to stash the cndrid properly later.

That will be your problem, not mine, he asserted. I need to sleep. He pressed a hand over his eye for nonverbal emphasis.

The way Huras's eyes squinted and his mouth quirked emanated frustration, as if a younger Quartermaster had whined, "Why do I have to do all the work?" He blinked several times and the impression was gone, Huras hefting him up with his usual unpleasantly neutral expression and only saying something about getting him back both fast and safely.

He had never been able to read a thought so clearly from another person's body language before. Had he simply learned to decode Huras's expressions, or had he actually heard a thought from another person's mindhome? Unnerved, he remained silent the entire return trip through the hallway and garden, glancing between Huras and various parts of the endless void the entire way.

Chapter 12

The day-cycles passed smoothly and began to blur together. Tzeldea had not been pleased with his overstimulation and had strictly restricted the time and intensity of activities he did outside his room. Huras drifted in and out, letting his padscreen provide the translation services more often than not and disappearing to work on the stolen cndrid. Since they'd taken it, Huras and he had mutually realized that an engineering cndrid would be their best chance at understanding how to activate blink and leave Dawi, especially with its similarity to the original cndrid Huras had been hacking on GU-T64A. Most of his attempts to join the decoding process had resulted in reaching into the void and blacking out, so he begrudgingly turned his focus onto Tzeldea's program of healing.

Today Tzeldea was taking him on his scheduled outing to the Eating Garden, this time substantially before the heavy traffic of the meal hours. Apparently patients and their assigned doctors habitually rotated shifts in various maintenance tasks such as preparing the food, cleaning, or operating technology to double as both necessary work and physical and emotional fulfillment while healing. It was time for his and Tzeldea's gardening shift, and he was finally recovered enough to cope with the sensory input and make the journey under his own power.

See here in the west corner, Tzeldea said with a smile, orange robes swishing as she swung her arms at her sides. These are the seedlings who must yet grow without winds. Once they have grown tall and strong and true, we will plant them in the orchards of the Jungle Fields. Slowing, she crouched by a tender still-green sapling and cupped its waxy feathered leaves in her hands.

Begrudgingly, he felt interest stir as he looked on the orderly spaced rows of various species interleaving between each other. He recognized smaller forms of the chlorophyll spikes from GU-T64A on one side five paces away, and he suspected the tree Tzeldea was cupping was a younger version of the one with the pink bulbous fruit. Several parasitic vines were growing along trains carefully wrapped around stronger saplings, and there was even some small foliage indicative of an edible geophyte.

"So many undocumented plants." It was a pity he had never been able to catalogue the bioflora and fauna on GU-T64A, the planet that he had last been together and whole. The void throbbed dully and he looked away.

What are we supposed to do? he said, setting down the odd woven basket full of their lunch, two trowels, and a pair of what looked like bamboo chopsticks. For all his expertise in botany, he specialized in exploration and what little he had had been mostly lost to the throbbing void.

Tzeldea exhaled long and steady on her cupped plant and sat back on her heels, spreading her hands in a gesture that he was beginning to recognize as one of acceptance or agreement. You have learned much about the soul, have you not? Even those without hearts can benefit from our honest care and love. We must check the seedlings and uproot any contrary sproutings, but most importantly we must offer them a watering of love. Your soul's scabbing will also come that much closer.

A half-remembered learning module flitted through his memory: some old, well-known rule to only talk positively while in greenhouses, especially those producing essential crops. He mentally tilted his head at the dual interpretations, his physical head unintentionally following suit. It was getting easier and easier to merge his mindhome actions with his physical reality. He wrinkled his nose and pointedly turned his focus back to Tzeldea and her actions.

She was murmuring over her cupped hands, smile evident and intent even as the padscreen carefully secured at his side by a blank blue sash buzzed the translation. You are loved, small one, and you will grow strong and true, your tzegea will clothe the backs of our people and Demaniwel will smile down upon us.

He slowly squatted as well beside the neighboring seedling, listening nonplussed to try to create a template for "offering a watering of love".

After about 15 seconds, she pulled away, settling back on her heels once again. Now it is your turn, she said, smoothing her robes and brushing off beads of dew from the sprinklers far above. Do not be afraid. The method does not matter, only your words and the heart behind them.

Blankly, he stared at the identical feathered seedling before him. The closest analogy to this task he had been able to think of so far was when he had been taught the technique of words of affirmation, and it seemed inconceivable to compliment the innate characteristics of a plant. He gingerly copied Tzeldea's original position and tried to dredge up appropriately loving statements to speak at his feathered sapling regardless, since he had come up with no better ideas.

You... are an above adequate plant. Your leaves are growing quite nicely according to my estimates of your age and taxonomical family. His mind drew a blank and he glanced longingly at Artist's nonexistent corner of the mindhome. This was supposed to be his kind of opportunity for creativity and emotional intelligence. Heart twisting, he turned his focus back on the unassuming green seedling. Its leaves quivered, tickling the palms of his hands. He loosened his grip and examined the plant as a whole instead.

Uh... Your leaves seem more than waxy enough to prevent rot from setting in despite the moist environment? Your stalk is strong, though it shows signs of far more flexibility than I would expect for a tree that is meant to grow in an environment full of strong and harsh winds. Are you an import to Dawi? The chlorophyll spikes are likely imports from previous planets, but I have no context for you as a "tzegea" fruit bearer...

Are you interested in the study of plants? Tzeldea asked, interrupting his muttering.

He jolted, hastily pulling his hands away so he would not damage the still tender plant. Tzeldea cocked her head at him, eyes crinkled, and he flushed and mentally kicked himself for getting absorbed enough to be startled so quickly. The question sunk in then and his embarrassment shifted to melancholy, dimming his budding excitement. Yes. It was my living, once.

Miscellaneous insect noises and rushing water filled the brief silence before the padscreen completed its translation. Thankfully Huras had pulled himself away from hacking the cndrid long enough to significantly shorten the delay time between translations. Without Scholar or Quartermaster, all the expertise he had once had was now lost to the emptiness inside him.

Tzeldea's posture softened and she came back around the planter, crouching down beside him. Would you like to have a lesson, then?

He thought of Leader nodding firmly and Scholar drooling at getting an insider's information, and the socialization experiments he had long since had to turn into his reality. His head ached and he wished all over again that the rest of him had never been swallowed by the void. The plants stood in front of him, waving gently in the barely perceptible ventilation breeze. Yes, he whispered, I would. It was the least he could do for Scholar and Quartermaster's memory.

Tzeldea ghosted a hand across his shoulder before moving back to the sapling she had first complimented. This is the gabin tree. You can tell by its wide water-shedding leaves and its rapid growth, as in the jungle it rapidly shoots up to break through the canopy and drink in the sunlight. It can grow taller than this solarium within ten years, though in the winds of Dawi it usually requires some support. If grown well, it produces tzegea fruit every three years, which is both fragrant and necessary for feeding the meri worms who spin our clothes.

She straightened and spread an arm toward a spindly orange-tinged tree laden with bulbous pink fruit. Look at the spiral-barked tree by the fountain there. That is a flowering gabin tree.

It has fruit on it, though, he objected. You gave it to me weeks ago. It is a hesperidium with many segments and a distinct citrus taste.

Tzeldea flicked her hand sideways in disagreement and crouched by the gabin seedlings again. It may have fruit, but the gabin tree is flowering. Like the blue citrus, the gabin tree bears false fruit in between its productive years, sating the hungry and nourishing the ground upon which it falls. We call them binam, because the flowers break through the skin once the false fruit ripens enough. Binam but not tzegea fruit are good to eat.

"Blue citrus! So they are related." The mindhome flared with triumph as his long-niggling suspicion finally fell into place. His hand twitched toward Huras's padscreen before he caught himself and settled for caressing a taller gabin sapling instead. False fruit from which flowers bloomed...That was certainly a unique method of propagation.

His brow furrowed. Did he know of any other species that created such false fruits, or was this a discovery deserving of a Sicntia submission proposing a reclassification or even the creation of a new genus? From what remained of his memories, he was fairly sure the Libet lemon would count, but the whole point of Scholar's sample expedition was to discover more about the blue citrus. With the addition of the gabin tree, he'd need at least one more species from an unrelated planet for a strong proposal—

He cut himself off. Constructing a mental proposal was pointless, especially since he as yet had no way to return to civilized space. Huras's padscreen wouldn't let him take the necessary pictorial documentation to support the addition of the gabin tree, and—he skated the unravelled edges of Quartermaster's void—he didn't remember how to formulate a reclassification proposal any more. Sudden emotion clogged up his throat and he swallowed repeatedly, withdrawing his hand from the sapling and looking away.

Do you grieve for the parts of yourself not here with you? Tzeldea asked, pausing over a chlorophyll spike and a parasitic vine.

He nodded, the silence of the void pressing in on him and threatening to swallow him whole. He squeezed his hands in his robes, not caring that he was smudging dirt into the deceptively smooth cloth. When that didn't work and the darkness of the mindhome started to impinge on his physical vision, he whispered, No one answers any more. Every time I speak it's swallowed up by the— I can't see—

He felt hands on his shoulders gently pushing him to the ground. Breathe, a warm voice insisted, first unintelligibly and then in a calm automated translation. The void does not consume you. You have lost much, but there is still much to gain. Demaniwel is here with you.

Slowly, he gathered himself and the blindness receded. He opened his eyes and found himself staring at his lap, clutching Tzeldea's smooth cinnamon hands. Licking his lips, he opened his mouth to speak, but every thought he had died into silence before he could find or verbalize the words.

Tzeldea continued rubbing her thumbs over the backs of his hands, murmuring more half-translated comforts in ancient English and Dawihcn. He tensed his hands and looked imploringly at her, unable to do anything but broadcast pain throughout the mindhome. The void pressed ever closer around him, threatening to eclipse the world again. He'd spent too long focused on the outside, the mindhome was destabilized, but he would only lose more of himself if he gave in and looked inward—

What purpose do I have if my passions only threaten to undo me altogether? he gasped out, grabbing onto the emotional thought and twisting it into words before it too was swallowed. I can't even— I love plants, but— He made an involuntary noise somewhere between a sniff and a hiccup. Words failed him again and he dug his fingers harshly into Tzeldea's palms.

Oh, little one, Tzeldea sighed and gently removed her hands from his grasp. Instead, she put one to his chin and tilted his head up to look at her face and the larger world around them. You grieve. That is well with you. But you do not have to stay in it forever. Live in love and enjoy your passions in their memory instead of as a constant reminder of your loss. Look beyond the void of your pain. There are stars among us, if you care to reach out to them.

CHAPTER 13

"Look up."

He was standing in the mindhome, darkness pressing in around him everywhere he turned. Void, nothingness, the vast emptiness of space, silence swallowing every call where there was once hint of light. But then, beyond the border where even the mindhome ended in its barrier against unattached minds, there was Tzeldea standing in her doctor's robes with hand outstretched. She was glowing like a star and an indistinct cloud of light hovered behind her.

He stared, thoughts stuttering and confusion and pain swirling around him like one of Scholar's rare storms in the mindhome. The safe space he stood on grew dimmer, but he could not take his focus from Tzeldea's impossible appearance. He'd hardly even begun to hypothesize about extra-mental spaces before the rest of him had been murdered, and now indisputably experiential proof stood in front of him, comfortably navigating beyond the void.

Tzeldea's shoulders slumped and a sigh stretched across the gap between them, coated with compassion. "Oh, little one, your burden is heavy. Will you let me take some of the pain?" Her intention came clearly, clearer even than Artist's own communication within the mindhome had sometimes been; she thought him little as one who was thrust into an overwhelmingly large world, floundering among stimuli he did not know how to interpret. He was a seedling choked in the jungles, light-starved and suffering from transplant shock, and she was a gildem frond reaching down to let the sunlight through.

"How are you doing this?" he whispered, turning the foreign thoughts and sensations over in his hands. "I'm— We're not attached minds now, are we? You said reforming the mindhome was impossible."

"This is Demaniwel's way," Tzeldea answered, dipping her head, the light shining brighter behind her. "He is always with us, so we can share in each other's burdens. This is the way of speaking between hearts, so we are not alone. Will you let me share some of your weights?"

Heart. She sent her intentions, and by 'heart' she meant the essence of one's being, focusing on matters of the spirit and soul. Mindhome to mindhome? The implications spun outward in seven hundred and twenty one different directions. "Can you do this with just anyone? What do you mean by 'no matter the time'?"

Tzeldea settled herself down so she was floating cross-legged beyond the mindhome barrier, hand still outstretched. "I can call, but you may not answer. It is common to reach out to those who do not see and receive no reply. Thus you may call and send thoughts, emotions, and intentions, but the other may not hear or discern that you are the source. But when you answer, your burdens can be shared like you as a zoldiwe shared one mind and heart."

Pain swirled around him, constricting his chest and choking his breaths somewhere out in the physical world. The void and Tzeldea beyond the mindhome took most of his focus. One of his and Scholar's burning recurring questions rolled into his memory, sliding into place with a combination of satisfaction and acute loss. "Is this how non-hiveminds form emotional connections?"

"Yes." Tzeldea's eyes sparked and her quiet happiness rolled into him. "The people of Demaniwel are all joined thus, though some connections are stronger than others. You could learn to live again this way, if that is what you desire." She sent impressions that were more emotion than concept, those of a large interconnected family spreading across the ages with someone always ready to listen, send comfort, or lend a helping hand. "You do not have to always be alone."

The void yawned around him, aching with the scabbed edges that had not yet turned to scars. Leader would urge him to take hold of this chance, to move beyond complete disability and live well in honor of his memory. Scholar would tell him that this was an unprecedented opportunity to finally connect with other minds, to probe the worldviews and motivations he had never been able to understand.

He took a step back and his fists clenched, tears leaking from his eyes and floating suspended like the heart-numbing drops of blood had been sprayed in the mindhome. Quartermaster would point out that he and Huras were planning to leave, that any emotional connections here would be temporary at best, external weaknesses at worst. And Artist... He would say to do whatever is best.

"I'm so tired of being alone," he cried out, mindhome dim with the prospect of yet another existential crisis, yet another world-altering choice. "I'm not the one who's supposed to make all the decisions. How am I supposed to decide when I am just a shell of myself clawing my way back to pretending normalcy? Nothing will be the same ever again. I'm never going to be whole again." He sank to his knees and hugged himself in lieu of toppling into the darkness where supporting arms had used to be.

"May I share your burdens?" Tzeldea's soft, half-hummed voice and gentle intentions startled him badly enough he flinched onto the bloodstained mindhome floor. "Please. It hurts me seeing you in pain. Let me bear your griefs with you."

"What does it help?" he asked, black tendrils of despair picking at the edges of the mindhome and probing the void. "You're not me, and I'm not you. You're outside the barrier. At best, you can only feel empathetic emotions."

"Let me try, and you will see." She extended her hand again, glow pushing gently against the suffocating darkness of the void.

He lay on his back and stared into nothing, too raw to dare locking gazes with the emptiness and too tired to try forcing his focus back onto the physical world. "Fine, try then. I just wish the rest of myself were here." Tears masquerading as blood drops hovered around him, screaming their own echoes that sped into the void and were lost.

Artist would be hugging him right now, in the mindhome and perhaps physically, and Leader would long since have ordered him off duty to recuperate in the nearest base with at least Artist and himself. Scholar would be running a constant unimportant informational monologue in the background, keeping him from being further distracted by the rest of his sensory input. Quartermaster would continue managing the mission and send a constant stream of support, and he would fall asleep smothered and content under the layers of focused attention in the mindhome. The next day-cycle he would be fine and Hirizcn would call in with a checkup or another mission report, and life would continue as normal.

He tried thinking of nothing and just floating in numbness for an indiscernible time, but the remnants of Scholar's voice told him he was probably in disassociation or shutdown, and Leader's sense of duty wouldn't let him consciously and willingly ignore such flagrant self-care violations. Begrudgingly, he sat up, studiously avoiding acknowledging the bloodstains, void, or teardrops in the mindhome and shifting his focus to his physical breaths, his heartbeat, and finally the soft metallophone music that was once again playing in the Eating Garden outside.

Tzeldea's hand was warm and heavy on his shoulder, and when he looked over her eyes were closed and her face was creased in some emotion adjacent to pain. He was too tired and wrung out to bother categorizing it. He let her continue "sharing his burden" and blinked, realizing that his tears had once again escaped physically and had now dried almost stickily on his cheeks. His nose wrinkled and the familiar gesture brought a flash of pain that quickly faded to a dull ache.

Strange. Rousing himself a little, he skimmed the edges of his emotions without turning his focus fully into the mindhome. All the tiredness, overwhelm, despair, sadness, anger, and pain were still there, but their intensities were faded now, dimming more as he watched in a slow but discernible and steady stream. What was she doing? How— how come she was able to drain his emotions?

Tzeldea's breath hitched, and he watched wide eyed as a single tear slid down the curve of her cheeks. She opened one eye and gave a wan smile, murmuring, I weep with you, little one. Is it that strange?

Why do you care? he blurted, something that used to be the core of his role driving him to understand. Why do you go to such lengths to heal me? I'm not an asset to you. I could have died and been none the wiser at the beginning. I'm an active danger to your civilization potentially being found. I'm nothing. No one. Why are you so determined to weep with me?

He felt the answer in the mindhome before Huras's padscreen translated her next words. Every heart is precious, whether zoldi-we, foreign, broken, or whole. I have love enough to pour into you as well as into others and those with whom I rejoice in my soul. Those whom she knew, whom she understood and was friends with, those with whom she shared an emotional connection just as deep and as rich as the understanding he all had shared united within the mindhome.

Years of quiet observation from Quartermaster clicked into place, and Leader's remnants inside him urged, Move on. Emotional connections were out there, if he wanted to reach out and find them. He traced a finger over the pale yellow cobblestone beside him, packing up his thoughts and memories and nestling them inside his mental projection of himself. He all would not have wanted him to remain alone forever, not even to protect himself from further deterioration or harm on future missions. Even a brief reprieve was better than an endless void of silence.

But to be with minds, he had to be known, and to be known, he had to have an identity for himself. Quietly, gently, tone so light and careful he feared the words would break, he asked, What is the word for Speaker in your language?

Tzeldea hummed softly, repeating the first few phrases of the song she had sung when they had first left. Zbigu, she enunciated, equally soft and gentle. Why?

That is what you can call me, he started, then stopped and tried again. He had to commit and lean into this new forming concept of himself. Gabin seedling leaves rustled under the beginnings of a hydrating mist. I mean, that is my name. I was the Speaker, once. I guess Zbigu is all I am left, now.

Chapter 14

W hy, he huffed as he braced his back against a glossy mirror and pried at a curved section of the geometrically tiled ceiling, did you decide the best place to hide the cndrid was the bathroom ceiling of all places?

For the same reason kids hide inside couch cushions when playing fugitive, Huras harrumphed, working his hand into the newly opened gap and lifting the section carefully onto the equally detailed floor. It's sneaky, there's more space than it looks like, and it's so obvious no one bothers to even check it any more. Now lift that pipe and move over so I can take the cndrid out.

He—Zbigu, he'd have to keep reminding himself until this new identity actually became even somewhat natural—obediently lifted the flexible pipe that was ostensibly part of the plumbing and frowned, trying to reconcile Huras's metaphor with reality. I don't see how this is obvious.

Huras grunted as he maneuvered himself into leaning on one edge of the gap on the ceiling and fished in the depths for the cleverly-camouflaged off-yellow cndrid. Figures. I forgot you'd have been a sheltered company brat. Did you ever watch the infamous Last Rcsistcnse bathroom scene? You'd be in the right age bracket for when that came out. He slid the cndrid out from the tangle of yellow, black, and red wires and began pulling it toward him.

What does entertainment have to do with the blatancy of hiding places in children's games? Zbigu asked, now utterly lost. When the mindhome first formed, he all had had to give up playing fugitive before he had started as there was no point hiding from himself when there was a constant stream of sensory input in the mindhome.

Well— The cndrid's arm clicked an obviously taped panel in the pipe he was holding and the maintenance valve started loosening on its own. Zbigu hurriedly angled the pipe away from the cndrid and Huras swore, yanking the cndrid out and tucking it protectively to his chest as he tumbled onto the floor. The valve clicked and water burst outward, spraying all over the bathroom floor.

Metal-warping deathwaste in the deepest virus of my navigation computer, Huras wheezed as Zbigu scrambled to reach the valve and close it off again. I swear this planet's plumbing has a vendetta against me.

Zbigu looked down at Huras, hunched over the open-backed cndrid like a protective mother mammal, hair dripping into his face and once again soaking wet, and couldn't suppress a snicker. You know, you were wet when I met you on GU-T64A as well.

Then this civilization's plumbing has a vendetta against me, Huras amended and attempted to give him a soggy glare. The action only intensified the pitiful mother mammal image and Zbigu's snickers turned into full on half-gasping snorts. Through his laughter, he double-checked the valve's tension and sank down onto the counter, still snickering.

It's not that funny, Huras grumbled. Now get down here and help me clean up before someone walks in on this steaming mess.

He snickered a few more times before hopping to the floor and shifting into business mode, forlornly ignoring the dead echoes where feedback from Leader and Quartermaster should have been. What do you want me to do, though? It's not like you brought any blow driers or water absorbers, and I can't be too involved in reverse engineering the cndrid coding. He clenched his hand behind his back and made sure his feelings on the matter stayed inside the mindhome and did not make it onto his face.

There's absorbents in the utility closet around the corner, Huras said, gingerly picking himself up and hefting the cndrid out of the danger zone. And I want you to be my plastic duck.

"Quack," he—Zbigu—said sardonically into the void, physically turning away and running a hand along the dark blue line that would lead to the utility closet. He resisted the Artist-style urge to kick his feet when he escaped Huras's line of sight. He had hardly any of Scholar or Quartermaster's coding-related knowledge any more, and the lack of expertise burned almost more than the embarrassment of being reduced to a near-passive observer.

The walk-in closet door was open and he grabbed a bucket of absorbents and a tool he assumed was Dawi's equivalent of a mop, movements short and sharp. When he almost slammed the bucket into the wall by his turn speed, he forced himself to stop and take a few calming breaths. Critically, he looked over his emotions. Shame, frustration, anger, the ever-present grief, and...fear.

"I am a different person now," he told himself firmly, "and I won't overreach and lose more of myself again." Then, before Huras could get suspicious, he speedwalked back to the bathroom and began briskly mopping up the plumbing mess.

He felt more than saw Huras look him over and decide he was emotionally stable enough to continue. Water splattered into the sink and technology clinked as Huras finished wringing his sleeves out and connected his padscreen to the cndrid, powering it on.

So, I've more or less deciphered the old programming language by now, especially with my old notes, Huras began, folding his legs and hunching comfortably against the driest section of the wall. I'm pretty sure I've managed to manufacture credentials so I can bypass rather than disable all the firewalls. Not that there are that many, to begin with. This civilization is absolutely idiotic about their security, but it works in our favor.

Zbigu dunked the mop into the absorbents, waited till the water had been mostly removed, and started on the second large puddle on the orange- and yellow-patterned floor. Healing and transportation, Tzeldea had explained to him the other day-cycle. Apparently the design told you that this was a bathroom.

So now I'm looking at the ship repair routines. There's the dimensional decoupling equation with several dozen warnings about potential missolution errors in their...I think this would translate to frozen drives? Whatever. Their FTL engines that solve for time rather than space, which I still don't understand how that works. He saw Huras stab his padscreen out of the corner of his eye. The second puddle dried up and he dunked his mop into the absorbents again.

Surprisingly they don't have nearly as many failsafes for dimensional stability or life support routines programmed into this system. Instead there's five entire pages dedicated to determining ship alloy structural integrity and stability over a range of— 500,000 years?! Not even titanqeel alloys are graded to last that long!

Now that was too ridiculous of a statement to ignore. He searched for words for a moment before verbalizing the most pertinent thought. All the civilization's ruins in the Plciadcs are both remarkably old and in remarkably good condition. It stands to reason that if they build their ships out of the same materials the longevity would be comparable. He couldn't count the number of times he all had taken shelter in remarkably untouched house ruins on one exploration mission or another.

But 500,000 years? That's insanity. Huras's gestures told him all he needed to know without even bothering to look at his face. You must be misremembering about all those ruins.

I wrote 617 reports in or around those ruins! he snapped back, restraint failing and lashing out of the mindhome. Just because I suffer memory loss doesn't mean all of my previous knowledge is unreliable. The city on GU-T64A alone should have long been swallowed with the climate and humidity of the rainforest's conditions. I may have lost my technical expertise, but I still have botany. Get over your corporation biases and figure out why Dawi's civilization is so focused on longevity. He clamped his mouth shut and screamed into the mindhome before Artist's temper could send him into another full on argument or spiral into spitting vitriol that he did not really mean.

Longevity, valuing longevity over speed, Huras muttered and trailed off, sounding disgustingly thoughtful rather than contrite. Inwardly he made a Leader-style bet with himself whether Huras would realize that he needed to apologize at all.

Huras slammed his fist into the counter and made a pressure cooker noise. Aha! How did I not recognize this sooner? Their protocols don't make sense because this is not FTL at all. Brain-addled weasel I am, Prof always told me not to get caught up in my own assumptions. Stupid, stupid, stupid! It all makes sense now. Ignoring Zbigu's startled glare, he descended into a coding fugue and started rapidly entering commands into his padscreen.

Chapter 15

Zbigu's curiosity warred with his simmering fury until the final puddle was dried up and the bucket and mop were ready to return to the utility closet. He was sure Scholar and Quartermaster would want to interrupt Huras or at least attempt to determine his realization so he could come to his own conclusions, but he did not want to break Huras out of flow and Artist would want to stomp away until he had worked through more of his emotions.

His mental simulation of Leader folded his arms and would not answer, and he wrinkled his nose, remembering that Tzeldea had told him to try to rely on his own judgments, not on what the rest of him would or would not have done. He took the bucket and mop to the door, wavered, and leaned them against the wall, deliberately taking several long screams into the void before pulling back and warily approaching Huras to look over his shoulder.

Huras did not even twitch, inputting commands and switching windows so quickly Zbigu's eyes blurred trying to follow the flurry of activity. Two columns of code scrolled by, one in Dawihcn symbols and one in the Gatik standard code he had once been fluent in. He caught and matched a few words on the screen from Huras's muttering: Stasis, for loop, else initiate protocol—, reverse function, emergency shutdown, maximum capacity. His head started to hurt from the influx of information as he struggled to assemble a coherent picture of what Huras was deciphering.

Pacing, he started verbalizing his thoughts in the mindhome. "He said it 'isn't FTL at all'. What's that supposed to mean? Longevity, time stasis technology, capable of transporting us 10,000 light years away in the blink of an eye. The cndrid is likely plasma powered with electricity moving out from the core, which gives another point to longevity and stability over maximum efficiency.

"What does time stasis have to do with non-FTL travel? Without FTL speeds it takes millenia to reach even relatively close systems, let alone distances at the range this civilizations' ships have been proven capable of." As the flow of his thoughts increased, he walked faster, waving his hands as he paced tight circles inside the mindhome. "Longevity. Slower than light travel. Time stasis. Somehow the three are connected. It seems to be a one-way trip and Huras's ship was lost in the process."

Finally the bolt struck him and he stopped short before starting up again, thinking faster than ever. "The ship was lost in the process! With the limitations of bounding a dimension decoupling, the ship must be being used as a container rather than being caught up within the stasis caused by solving the equation for time.

"That means whatever means of transportation they use to travel such distances doesn't bring the ship because it's the container that determines what is sent where. Since time is the independent variable, space is the factor being moved, which means at some point the ships must indeed arrive at the destination but it is not necessarily the moment their time-frozen cargo arrives at the destination—"

He took a step too far and his foot slipped into the void. He yelped, twisted, pulled at a frayed edge that only sent a bolt of pain into his reeling mind—

Pain swamped him from all sides and he was staring at blood in the mindhome. What? But Tzeldea had said he had been progressing in healing nicely. He reached out to Leader to ask him what was going on—

His thoughts were fragmented and fractured and his physical sight was jerking up and down, and he couldn't understand why. The engineer was in his face and the ceiling behind him was a different pattern than the one that was in his room. Huras was wet again and his voice was twisted into urgency that made no sense against the pounding in his ears.

He heard himself mutter, "I know where Huras's ship is," felt the fading flutters of excitement and satisfaction over the prevailing currents of mental and emotional pain, and realized there was blood sprays suspended in the mindhome. Had he fallen into the void again? He put a hand to his head—mentally or physically?—and slitted his eyes, trying to restore coherency to his thinking.

Huras was saying something, and he thought he could detect fear in it, which was odd since he had been pretty sure Huras still strongly disliked him. How much memory had he lost this time? The words inside and outside the mindhome jumbled and he resorted to using pictorial rather than verbal thoughts.

He'd been clenching his fists with anger about something, and before that he'd watched Huras get wet, and there was a picture of GU-T64A with a lot of asteroids departing from it, wreathed in realization and triumph? He wasn't sure how that connected, but at least it seemed like the trend toward losing less and less memory as time progressed was still holding strong, thankfully.

"Speaker, don't you dare die!"

The sudden voice echoed and he—Speaker, Zbigu, hadn't he made a decision about which name he was going by internally?—jumped, getting a bloody faceful and shuddering even as he whirled around, searching for the voice that had escaped the void.

His eyes landed on Huras and he stared, blurting the first verbal thought that came to him. "How do you know that— my— that name?"

"Now you're listening?" Huras scoffed, fear still bleeding off of him in waves. "I asked for the translation ages ago. Stop erasing yourself with your own mind!"

Speaker frowned, casting glances at Huras's position in between wiping the blood off his face. "I didn't do it intentionally, I don't think. Also, I think I know where your ship is."

Huras gritted his teeth, flashes of hospitals and halting life support flickering across the gap between them. "Intentionally or not, I don't care. You're coming back to your bed and you're staying there from now on. I can figure out this virus-ridden bit of machinery myself."

Zbigu felt himself physically hauled to his feet and stumbled, one arm caught and one hand out for balance as his inner ears swirled in protest. He saw a mop and a bucket and had the passing thought that he needed to stop and put it away. "But your ship!

You're a captain, captains always are sensitive about not knowing where their ship is."

"My ship's somewhere in the Clacnu system and I can't get it back without inducing a temporal paradox," Huras said bitterly, dragging him out the bathroom door and down the quiet hallway that led to the Eating Garden. "I'll figure out what I'm going to do about losing my livelihood once we get back into known space. You stop concerning your idiotically nosy self about it and figure out how to stop killing yourself by accident!"

Any further attempts at conversation were lost as the Eating Garden's chaotic combinations of sights, sounds, and smells smashed through his scrambled mind's defenses, and it was only several hours after Huras had returned him to his room and he had gotten a long, biting lecture from Tzeldea did Zbigu realize what had been strange about that entire interaction.

He had had an entire conversation with Huras across the border of the mindhome. He had made an emotional connection with his murderer.

Chapter 16

What are the other parts of your heart like, Zbigu? Tzeldea asked over pickled binam and rais with curry that strangely left no spice tingling in his mouth.

Zbigu ducked his head and swallowed, pushing away his reflexive urge to shut down on his outward expressions and refuse eye or emotional contact. Despite his fifth relapse, Tzeldea had finally deemed him ready to proceed with the 'healing of his soul', and processing his grief with her was supposed to be a part of it. He hated the concept of revealing something so personal to any other mind, but it was not like he had other options, and he had kept more than enough memories of self-care lectures that he knew in the end it was for the best.

He allowed himself one nose wrinkle and one moment of petty grousing before forcing himself to turn over how to answer her question in earnest. I... There were five parts of me in all. Each of me liked different things and had different specializations, but together I was one beautifully efficient whole. I hardly ever fought with myself, not after my long years of specialization and experience, except for the moments right before the blink. His voice caught at the memory of Leader's assertions that he would handle it, and that it had been safe for him to finally go to sleep.

But who were they? What are the things that you grieve most about the parts of your heart? Tzeldea pressed. You have told me what you were together, but not what made up each part. If you help me understand, I may be able to help teach you more closely to what is already clear to you. Flicking her fingers, she took another bite of her rais and curry and tilted her head in the way that he had learned meant she was waiting for him to continue.

Zbigu took a deep breath, skimmed a finger over all his most precious memories, and started with Quartermaster. The practical one liked getting all the numbers and logistics straight. I couldn't stand trusting other minds not to be sloppy or forget to check all my equipment, so I appointed the job to myself and discovered I liked it. I also had a good head for decisions, but... He looked at his emotions and cringed at the discord they should have made in the mindhome.

Hunching his physical shoulders, he told himself firmly that he was doing this to become a functional person and functional individuals regularly shared embarrassing confessions to those they called their friends. Was Tzeldea a friend? Perhaps not, but the only other person he had so far shared an emotional connection with was Huras and he certainly wasn't going to share vulnerable emotional secrets about the dead parts of himself to his murderer. I was one of the closest to me in the mindhome, and I made sure I was never isolated or overwhelmed inside the mindhome. You know how I am about sensory input now.

Tzeldea reached across the table and held his hand, squeezing gently without preventing him from slipping away. You are doing better than you know, Zbigu, she said, gazing steadily at him until he caved and made eye contact. Your heart is hurting, but you are listening and do not turn the rest of your soul away.

"What's that supposed to mean?" he grumbled to himself, but quickly turned his focus outward and away from the depressingly dark and empty space in the mindhome. Then there was the assertive one. That part of me also took Speaking duties, sometimes, but I preferred to be the main coordinator so that all of me could stay focused on my varied time-sensitive jobs. I was the one who had a tendency to get so caught up in organizing the rest of me that I just stood there physically and forgot to take part in the mission myself.

He took a bite of pickled binam and swallowed, wracking his safe memories for what about Leader he missed most. I always made all the important decisions. It's overwhelming to learn how to live without it.

Tears pricked at the corners of his eyes and a low ache started to rise in the mindhome. Breaking eye contact, he took a shaky breath and looked up at the gabin tree they were under, moving on before he could feel too much and get swept away. Then there was the most intelligent one. I was an insatiable learner with an eclectic range of subjects who the rest of me had to keep reminding to go to sleep instead of signing up for yet another learning module. I— I've lost most of my knowledge of that part of me now, more than any other part.

A phantom pain stabbed his heart and he gasped, curling over himself and resting his forehead on the cool stone table. The mindhome creaked with aborted calls outward, each word about the rest of himself sending echoes that would never be answered and tempting him to reach out and follow them into the vacant void.

Tzeldea hissed and hurried around the table, sliding in beside him and starting to rub comforting circles across his back. I am sorry, the padscreen translated a moment later, I see your wounds are as yet too deep to probe them all at once. Your other parts sound like vibrant souls. I suppose to you their brightness only makes the void all the darker, now.

How is this supposed to help? he breathed out between the realization that one day-cycle he might not remember anything of what Scholar was like at all. How does talking to other minds do anything other than crystalize unpleasant realizations and make my pain even worse?

Tzeldea was silent for a moment, making his own hitched breaths and the nearby rustling chlorophyll spikes all the more prominent. I do not know how best to explain it, the padscreen admitted eventually. Words have power. Speaking your pain often releases it so that your soul's river ceases flooding and the healing may begin. I regret that the process is slow and causes you more pain, but it is as lancing a lesion to release the overflowing discharge, especially as your mind still reaches out beyond its borders.

A few more beats of nothing, and then Zbigu felt a gentle knock on the border of the mindhome. The sensation still put him off, but he looked beyond the void to Tzeldea's glowing figure and sent his trembling sense of inquiry.

"Sometimes it is better to show you," she said and started directing the swirls around her into distinct pictures of light. "For those of us who have never shared hearts, there is no greater desire than that of being fully and completely known." One swirl solidified into a silhouette with a void inside the middle, and the other turned into another silhouette with the edges glitching and blurred out. "But without such communication to the depths of the soul, how can one be sure that your meaning is both fully sent and completely understood?"

Despite his grief, he perked up. Was Tzeldea going to answer one of the first and most opaque questions about unattached minds that Scholar had been able to conceptualize or answer? He leaned forward but stopped himself from moving and risking reaching out into the void.

Tzeldea sent quick approval and continued, waving her hands as if she was talking in the physical world and not the mindhome. "Without eyes to see it is near impossible to reach beyond yourself. At most, it is two hands grasping each other in the dark. The slightest storm can rip them apart." She did something with her fingers, and a shimmering bond sprung to life between the two silhouettes. Zbigu felt a pulse of half-remembered experiences, brief connections and shared emotions that faded outside of the moment. The void ached, but he could not turn his eyes away.

"Soul bonds such as those between friends, spouses, or beloved are stronger, but still..." The glowing bond snapped, the glitching silhouette disappearing and the hollow one doubling over in pain. A flash of his own death blitzed across his mind and he shrunk in on himself, fighting off another distracting spiral at even the imagined sensation of anything like the mindhome being ripped away.

Comfort and understanding drifted to him in the mindhome, tinged with resignation and a bone-deep ache that could only come from experience. Tzeldea smiled sadly and let the hollow silhouette disperse into the constant glowing around and behind her. "Like your mixed souls, a bond once broken does not easily grow skin over itself again."

He paused hugging himself and really looked at her, the layers of her words resonating strangely in the mindhome. That last comparison really did reek of emotions intense enough they could only be deeply personal. His chest twinged and he tensed his grip on himself, looking away from the darkness. "Who did you lose?"

Even without looking, in the strange way of Tzeldea's telepathic connection he saw her flinch and reflexively withdraw, a sharp blade of anger-pain-grief-hurt lancing across the barrier of the mindhome. But instead of distancing herself fully and removing her emotions from the connection, she let go of them and...they were just not potent anymore. Curiosity bubbled up and swirled around him, but he bit his tongue, trying to be considerate for once and not prod Tzeldea's trauma. It was the least he could do to be patient with her as she had been with him.

Tzeldea sighed and shifted to rest her hand on his left shoulder in the outside world. He felt her gather her thoughts, sift through some memories, and then breathe out her measured response. "My brother." With the words came a flurry of impressions: twin, other half, raised together, Tzeldea-and-Dazgu, taken suddenly in a ship-related accident, the ripping and bleeding and the desolation of her soul.

Zbigu reeled, his paradigms shifting once again as his own destruction was mirrored in another person's experience. His response was muted, painfully naive-sounding and reminiscent of Scholar's younger complaints. "I thought unattached minds had no concept of emotional connection, or devastation, like I do."

"We are not unattached souls," Tzeldea corrected, gently putting a hand against the metaphysical barrier of the mindhome, "and all souls bleed when those connections are broken. This is why Demaniwel's way is so precious to us."

CHAPTER 17

A shock of sudden wetness yanked Zbigu back into the external world, and his shame intensified further when he realized he had gotten so absorbed in the mindhome he had dropped his hand and utensil in his food. Pulling his emotions away so he could not possibly send them to Tzeldea, he hurriedly replied, And how does Demaniwel's way help? You talk about it but I don't see how it changes things. The rest of me is still gone.

Tzeldea mirrored his decision and shifted so she outwardly faced him, taking another bite of pickled binam and humming thoughtfully while she chewed. Demaniwel's way heals the deepest scars of the soul, she paused to let the padscreen translate before adding on quietly, Even me.

The last tonal inflection made him look up and more carefully take stock of Tzeldea's body language. For the first time since he had known her, unless he had lost something to the void, Tzeldea's hands lay still on the table, fingers tightly intertwined as she pensively frowned. His heart quickened as he catalogued her minute fidgets and unusually hesitant false starts to her next words and he realized she was about to initiate an interpersonally important moment in their conversation.

Once, long ago, Demaniwel came to take on all the scars of our souls, she said at last, cadence halfway between a legend long recited and her usual direct language. The morning light fell around her and painted chlorophyll shadow spikes across the table and the floor. *This was before any person had ever set foot beyond the stars.*

He blinked. This was an ancient story indeed. He guessed Demaniwel hadn't been the cultural figure of this civilization's splintering off after all.

Tzeldea broke his gaze and looked down, taking a calming breath before continuing. *He took all the pain and suffering our brokenness causes and poured it upon Himself, and caused Him to die.* Her voice wavered and he cocked his head, wondering whether her distress was because of the legend or the reminder of her dead twin brother.

After a moment and a discreet touch to the woven bracelet she always wore, she continued, stilted cadence dropping as she began to get into the flow. *But He did not stay dead. Because He is greater than all the scarring of our souls, Demaniwel rose, and He offers us a life that stretches beyond the boundaries of space and time. If we are in Him, and He is in us, we share a connection that knows no bounds and can never be broken.*

Among all who are in Him, even death is but a temporary disconnection before our eternal reunion. Again, Tzeldea touched her bracelet, tilting her hand so he could see the five-colored sigil on her inner wrist. *As He is alive, so we will be alive, so my soul's wounds are healed knowing that Demaniwel has taken them, and* that my twin brother will be waiting for me on that day-cycle that I too learn what it means to have a completely unshattered soul.

She finished and sat back with one of her gentle smiles, bittersweet but grounded in a way that, with the void, he was not sure he would be able to achieve. Zbigu withdrew and looked inward for a moment, turning Tzeldea's speech over in his mind. He'd never heard anything like this before, but with the way Tzeldea spoke he was pretty sure it was one of the ancient religions. Hirizcn had banned him from taking any extracurricular modules on the comparative or cultural aspects of religion, so even if he had lost memories Scholar had likely never known about this.

He couldn't deny the impact such beliefs have had on Tzeldea; even factoring out her general personality and the environmental lighting, she was practically glowing in front of him physically, smile soft and genuine even as she looked at what must have been a symbol of her dead brother and the ever-present absence in her mind. And internally, despite the pain he sometimes felt from her, she was also settled and at peace, shining like a star beyond the void of the mindhome.

A thought struck him. What about the rest of me? How would I ever reunite with myself if I would believe and follow in Demaniwel's way, but not the rest of me? I'm already dead, after all.

Tzeldea's head tilted and she spread her hands out in genuine confusion. Why would the other parts of you be dead?

Indignation and horrified fury instantly rose up and swept away his budding consideration of Tzeldea's ideas. He spat out his reply, pushing away his food and cutting the air, mindhome swirling in sudden betrayal and confusion. Why would I not be dead?! Since I was made I have never gone a day-cycle in my life without constantly feeling the thoughts and emotions of the other parts of myself in the mindhome, I've never been unable to reach out to the other parts of myself or found the mindhome adrift and empty, I've never been trapped in darkness or silence or fallen into the void, what do you mean?

Tzeldea raised her hands and leaned away, posture shuttering and falling into what he disgustingly recognized as attempting to be calm and soothing. His nose flared and he almost missed her answer in spitefully wondering whether she was more concerned about him or his loud outburst drawing the attention of others. Is your separation not from the dimensional travel and distance caused by the blink? I thought you would have learned this from your own records.

Permafrost manifested in the depths of the pitiless void and Artist's temper collapsed into Leader's cold, calculated, closely controlled fury. So you are saying that the other parts of myself are still alive. The background rustling swelled as if commenting on the sudden, heavy silence.

Tzeldea's shoulders tensed and she placed her hands against the table, muscles tight as she calmingly, warily answered, glancing at the padscreen while it translated. If they survived the shock of your sundering, yes.

Zbigu abruptly stood and stalked away, fists clenched and uncaring that he had abandoned his unfinished food. And you will not let me return to myself. Cloth scratched against stone and Tzeldea's footsteps hurried after him, melodic voice high and rushed in protest, but he held up a hand and cut her off, channeling every drop of Leader's diplomatic-packed poison into his delivery and tone. Don't worry, I understand. It's too dangerous for you to let me go back. You want me to form connections with you instead.

He stopped, every muscle clenched and full body trembling from the force of his emotions. Anger, hate, pain, grief, he didn't have enough control to be able to tell any more. He was alive, he was alive, according to all the odds he was mostly alive. His dubious mental restraint snapped and he whirled around to scream at her, sudden tears flooding in and blurring his eyes. Why didn't you tell me?!

He just caught a glimpse of Tzeldea's horrified and hurt face no more than five steps away before he flung his arm over his eyes and fled the garden, upset at his own meltdown only adding to the maelstrom blocking out all his rational thoughts in the mindhome. All this time he'd spent grieving and stretching and keeping himself on a tight leash and gradually coming around to Tzeldea's point of view, and it was all based on a trick. Manipulative liar, she'd known exactly what kind of ploys she'd needed to begin to forge a surrogate emotional connection and he'd fallen for it, believing she had been genuine all this time. Tzeldea of all people should have known that he would do anything to be whole with the rest of himself again.

A desperate cry sounded behind him as he narrowly swerved around a particularly twisted gabin tree and careened into the hallway that led back to his prison hospital room. Who knew if that was even true, if he had been there for his own benefit and healing rather than to keep him isolated and primed for external emotional connections. The padscreen's translation blared out behind him, doubtless being cranked up to full volume, but he blocked the words out by shouting over them, risking one brief call

over his shoulder so that his meaning could not be misunderstood.
I don't want to hear it! Leave me alone.

Chapter 18

Storming into his quarters, Zbigu threw himself to the ground and pulled out the storage unit underneath the bed. He hadn't had much on him when the blink had taken him away, but his scanner, Hirizcn uniform, and all-purpose boots had been so graciously returned to him by Tzeldea weeks ago. They'd have to be good enough for his escape attempt. He ripped off the blue inpatient robes and changed quickly, pausing just long enough to disgustedly pull the hospital gown over his clothes again. He'd better take advantage of his status for as long as he had left. The void throbbed and he stumbled, feeling blindly for the bed long enough to sit down and wait out the blackness threatening to swallow his vision.

He didn't have time for this. The deceiver might still be following him and he didn't— He couldn't— Making a strangled noise echoing half in, half out of the mindhome, he threw himself out into the hallway and traced the blue and orange strings that led to Huras's quarters. If anyone passed him in the hallways, he didn't notice, too caught up in focusing on his fury so that he could function outside the hurricane of the mindhome.

Is the cndrid ready? he snarled, bursting into Huras's dusky orange room and gripping his inactivated scanner with white knuckles.

Huras jerked and whipped his head up from where he was hunched over the deactivated cndrid's innards. Zbigu! What made you burst an engine and fly out of atmosphere? Aren't you supposed to be in your therapy session with Tzeldea?

Just answer the question, he growled, shifting his fingers just enough to let both eyes glare despite having a hand over his face. His head throbbed in time with his single heartbeat (he should be feeling five, he could be feeling five if Tzeldea had not lied to him), and he seethed as Huras clearly evaluated whether he was emotionally compromised.

Apparently the conclusion was yes as Huras straightened, nudging the more fragile carapace sections away from the entry before speaking with deliberately calm and quiet tones. I can probably get it to take us back home, but I'd need my padscreen. What's the big rush? I thought you were all hunky dory with the creepy telepathic methods they use here.

Tzeldea is a manipulative dissembler who was attempting to induce emotional dependence in me when she knew the rest of me was still alive and suffering back on that accursed GU-T64A, he spat, forcing his tone to stay angry and even and blinking away the treacherous tears that would betray his internal conflict. He instinctively grasped outward and just managed to remember Huras was not part of him and snatch himself back before he tumbled into the void. Forcefully, he relaxed his grip on the scanner and regulated his breathing. He was fairly sure he had not lost any moments in time.

Huras grimaced and made a commiserating grunt. That sucks. I'd still want more time to get a better error margin for these calculations before we attempt to hijack a spaceship, though.

I'm not spending a millisecond longer than necessary away from the rest of myself. It's already been weeks too long with the silence in the void, he hissed. His head hurt. Time was of the essence. How long would he have to wait before Huras would consider it safe enough for them to leave? You're a competent person. The error margins are good enough.

The compliment only made Huras look less sure, and after a charged moment he snorted, seized his arm, and began to drag him over to the rumpled bed. I'm not risking getting stuck outside the timeline because you got a little impatient. Lie down and get your head back on straight.

Zbigu struggled, finding leverage against Huras's grip just as he was unceremoniously dumped on the cream covers. The distinct smell of citrus and machine oil made him gag, strangling the delivery of his response. That is not the point. I'm not talking to that dissembler again and she always gives me space when I get into a state like this. This is our chance. Just grab your padscreen from her and let's go.

You sure you want to do that, ki—Zbigu? Huras stressed the Dawihcn name. The thing about angry partings is that you'll always regret never saying goodbye. Something clattered on the floor out of sight and Huras hissed an indistinguishable curse. A few moments later, he tossed out an afterthought. And I'm not budging. 15 percent margin or we don't go at all.

"You don't understand," he cried, anchoring himself desperately so that he would not fly into the void. "I have to find myself. I can't be— I'm on the verge of dying like this and that liar's emotional connections— There is no other way."

Distantly his fragmented logic told him that that did not negate Huras's valid concerns. He ground his teeth and resigned himself to placating the only engineer who would get him out of here. How long would you need to get 15 percent? I'm not staying here a moment longer than I have to.

He lifted his head long enough to see Huras grouchily roll his eyes. It takes as long as it takes. Debugging's slow work. A couple of hours, at the very least.

Impatience flared in his chest and shot out his mouth before he could filter it. Then work faster! Or do you care about going home to your wife and children at all?!

Huras drew back with a short gasp and looked for a moment like he was going to murder him. Regret spiked, but anger overrode his expression and he bared his teeth, daring the freelancer to make his previous title true. A myriad of complex expressions crossed the engineer's face before it shut down altogether and he turned away abruptly, leaving the room without a word.

Zbigu's breath came in short bursts, almost as fragmented as his conflicting thoughts. He felt furious at the liar for keeping secrets from him, vindicated that his guess about Huras's mysterious 'someone to get back to' had been correct, betrayed that emotional connections here had indeed been a liability biasing his judgment, angry that he had goaded Huras into leaving instead of helping, frustrated that he had so little emotional control, ashamed that he was so gullible without Leader's more cynical input, distressed because all the feedback would not stop pounding into the center of the mindhome, desperate to get back to the rest of himself so the pain would just stop—

Everything was so overwhelming right now. Without any better option, he curled into a ball and dug his hands into his skull, discovering he hadn't dropped his scanner in the process. Tears leaked from his tightly compressed eyelids and the distress he could not vent in the mindhome came out in whines rather than the counting of grounding breathing exercises. Minutes passed and he recognized his state enough to let himself cry like Artist had rather than attempt to keep it all inside. It was his only recourse when he was still only a crippled shell of himself.

The mindhome gradually calmed enough that he began to string together coherent verbal thoughts again. He'd been unfair to Huras. He'd been working practically nonstop all the time Zbigu had spent stumbling around like a newborn fawn and learning how to walk in the garden without being overwhelmed. What little he could remember of coding told him Huras had taken on a gargantuan task and made remarkable progress in the given timeframe, especially with the cultural and conceptual barriers involved. He'd have to apologize whenever Huras found fit to walk back into the room.

He physically stirred and wiped his face, grimacing at the mucus clogging his nose. Shakily uncurling and sitting up, he swiftly made his way to the bathroom and cleared his sinuses, keeping a hand to his head and avoiding concerned passerby's gazes.

He stopped short in the doorway of Huras's room, the engineer himself already crouched on the floor and hooking up his padscreen to the cndrid. Huras looked up flatly, mood clear by the lack of expression on his craggy face.

Suddenly remembering common etiquette, Zbigu shifted awkwardly and broke his gaze from Huras's face. What I said was uncalled for. You've been dedicated to returning since the beginning, he muttered, voice still croaky with tears. I just— The revelation shook me and I lashed out. I'm sorry.

Huras snorted and jerked his head dismissively, turning back to his padscreen lit up with varying windows of code. It's fine. According to Diqa I always needed a kick in the gut to get my priorities straight. Tzeldea's quite distraught about you leaving in a huff, you know. You should talk to her while I get these error margins done.

Anger and pain and betrayal immediately riled up again and Zbigu inhaled sharply, putting a hand back over his face. I can't, he finally gritted out when he had his emotions mostly under control. But if it makes you happy I'll leave a message.

Do whatever you want. Huras tapped a couple of buttons and opened a new coding screen. Half the text lit up red and he scrolled rapidly. But there's no network here. Good luck finding a pen and paper.

Zbigu shifted uncomfortably and stepped back into the room, sliding around Huras to settle once more on the unmade bed. Rather irritatingly, Huras had a point again. In all his memories of this civilization's complex he had not seen any use of physical writing materials. The only thing indicating they had them was the honest to goodness physical tome propped up in the corner. That was the equivalent of paper, but he had nothing to write with.

Wait, backing up a second. Did he really want to leave a message for Tzeldea, anyway? A pang of longing answered his preliminary poke at his emotions and he was forced to admit that some part of him still clung to his emotional connection with Tzeldea. He remembered the agony of being ripped apart in the void and all the articles of mental health and closure he—Artist? Quartermaster? He didn't remember—had read, and reluctantly concluded that he did.

That left the question of where to get a writing implement and what he was going to say. You lied to me. Your betrayal is everything Hirizcn had taught me to avoid. You of all people should know what it's like to lose everything. Why did you do it to me? No, no, that was just his anger speaking. This was going to be the last thing he said to her. What did closure mean if he had too many things to say?

Chapter 19

Two hours passed nearly silently as Zbigu internally debated on what to put in his final message. Huras made only a few deep concentration noises, interspersed with cut off sentences and the occasional firm thump on the intact carapace of the cndrid. He eventually settled on a brief but honest message: Thank you for all you have taught me, but I must be reunited with myself. You've shown me a lot about non-hiveminded beings. Signed, Zbigu. He hoped Tzeldea understood all the unspoken meanings he didn't know how to convey without the mindhome.

After that it was a quick moment to pop the lens of his scanner, adjust it to be even more tightly focused, and change the setting to a laser reader. He frowned down at the mechanism while waiting for Huras to be finished and provide a Gatik-to-English translation.

The more he thought about it, the more he realized that he did not really want to return to his strict no-attachment contract with Hirizcn. He'd found he'd rather come to like his peaceful and routine-based existence here on Dawi, despite the occasional itch to set out and explore more flora. He'd never had much to occupy him on the downtime between missions, and he'd never had the chance to settle down and really dig into the bioflora and fauna of one singular region or planet. It satisfied a long-aching feeling of purposelessness outside of his career. If Tzeldea's overtures had been genuine, he'd also felt acceptance and belonging that just had never been present outside of the mindhome.

The problem was that he was the only one here to enjoy it. The void yawned within him, and he wearily pulled himself back from the tattered edges. He had to find the rest of himself. He just had to hold out a little longer. Then everything would be alright again.

Done. Huras sat back with a satisfied smirk. Got your last words, Zbigu?

He nodded, wrung out and uncomfortably suspicious that he was forgetting something important, and recited his message. Huras handed him the padscreen, busily reassembling the cndrid and gathering his meager belongings while Zbigu painstakingly used the scanner to burn the words into the front page of the tome. The remnants of Quartermaster tapped his foot impatiently as he burnt letter by letter and hoped Tzeldea would not be offended by his defacing of the tome.

We'll have to track through the edges of the Eating Garden, Huras said, dumping a bag made of his knotted orange robe into Zbigu's arms the moment he finished. Walk quickly and pretend you're on laundry duty. I'll take the cndrid.

Understood. The mindhome lay quiet and tense with resolve as he adjusted his grip and led the way to the repair bay, following the yellow strings right to the Eating Garden and skirting by the seedlings he and Tzeldea had 'watered with love'. He stepped over a decorative stream with ease, but Huras had to stop and heft the cndrid with its multiple exposed panels with considerable difficulty. His boot slipped and splashed heavily in the stream, and Zbigu's amusement flared even as he hastily dropped his bundle to help Huras carry it safely across.

Thankfully, they made it across the gardens and into the engineering hallway without undue attention. The floor and ceiling gradually increased with yellow strands as the ground changed from cobblestone to tile to manufactured material. They passed the white string corridor to the laundry and Zbigu picked up his pace, knowing that his thin alibi was now flimsier than ever. Tendrils of fear skirted the edges of the mindhome, spurring him onward. If they were caught now, would he ever have another chance?

Two corridors. One. Huras barely rolled the cndrid into a kafii room in time to dodge a group of engineers coming down the hallway. The metallophone music signalling midday rung out from hidden speakers. Zbigu counted the seconds in his head, not daring to pace even tightly within the mindhome. With how frazzled he was he wanted no chance of accidentally incapacitating himself.

Huras leaned out the door and gestured for him to make a break for it. His indoors-setting boots sent slaps echoing down the hall, but he was through the firsficld and in the blast of acid fruit and machine oil and humid wind and behind the closest generator before he could wince at the stimulation of it all.

He took a moment to recenter himself, and when he blinked Huras was already halfway across the gap furiously rolling the cndrid to the nearest ship. Hastily, he checked no one was watching and sprinted after, ignoring the steadily building overwhelm in his head. He just had to make it onto the ship and Huras would take care of the rest.

Zbigu sighed in relief when they slid under the firsficld and the howling wind became muffled. He crouched, making sure the generator blocked him and Huras from the other ships' line of sight. Most of their engineers were finishing up and streaming toward one or more yellow marked doors, clothes flapping in the wind.

Huras pried a panel open, looked through the wiring, and shook his head shortly. Engine's down. Not this one.

Dismay curled his lips and he blurted, How many will we have to check?

This is a repair bay, frizz brain. Huras leaned around the generator and hastily jerked back to avoid a passing engineer. It takes as many as it takes.

The next three ships they checked were a blur of half-verbalized thoughts and blasts of sensory input. Finally they found a ship Huras deemed serviceable, and Zbigu stood watch as Huras searched for an access port to plug the cndrid into. Huras muttered something about mixed signals in the ship's design and Zbigu staggered in sudden revelation.

Your soul is too small to be mixed now. Zoldiwe cannot reform once broken, even with their original parts.

That was what he'd been forgetting. The mindhome throbbed and he set Huras's bundle down to press both hands over his eyes. He was such a liability like this. Had he been whole, he would never have forgotten something so important, mental overload due to the void or not.

He shoved his burgeoning despair down and firmly bit his lip. Even if Tzeldea was right, Hirizcn had many resources Dawi did not, and even the external support of the rest of himself would be a balm to his overwrought soul. He had to return, and if he wanted to back out, he was in too deep already. There was no choice but to press forward.

What if his time apart changed the mental makeup of the void, and the scarring prevented him from ever reforming together? What if he'd have to live alone surrounded by the rest of himself, always tempted to reach into the— Zbigu jerked his eyes open and his thoughts away to his current task. A circular cndrid was gesturing angrily at them and beginning to roll its way to the gap in the firsficld.

We've got company! he called to Huras, positioning himself in the entrance and desperately wishing he retained enough engineering knowledge to speed the hacking process along. Huras had the ship's belly open and was struggling to find a port to connect the cndrid to. He nudged the bundle a little farther aside and alternated glances between the engineer and the rapidly approaching cndrid.

The second cndrid stopped in front of Zbigu and beeped furiously, attempting first to outmaneuver him, then to push him aside. He dug his feet and tried to stand his ground, but the cndrid was relentless and he had nowhere near the strength to resist engine-driven wheels. How much longer are you going to take? he called to Huras, switching tactics and beginning to lead the cndrid in a game of feline and rodent.

Not much longer. I'm only reverse engineering cutting edge technology here, Huras snarked back, stance tense despite his flippant tone. Zbigu feinted toward the firsficld and got the cndrid to shock itself into shutdown just as Huras grunted and the ship's ramp finally began to lower. Got it!

The two of them hurriedly disconnected the hacked cndrid and pushed it up the ramp, Zbigu darting down to grab the bundle as Huras reconnected the cndrid and began to run the ship-warming protocols. When he checked outside to see whether they had attracted notice, Zbigu saw several engineers turning and gesturing disgruntled from several ships over. Ducking back inside and shifting from foot to foot as Huras rapidly ran set after set of commands, he said urgently, We're running out of time.

Give me a few more seconds, Huras bit out, mouth working and brow furrowed in concentration over his padscreen.

Zbigu began to pace and kept checking the situation outside, barely keeping himself from nagging as the engineers left their posts and came over to investigate. "Come on Huras," he muttered, folding his arms tightly and resisting pacing in the mindhome, "Don't fail us now."

Chapter 20

Got it! Huras stabbed the padscreen triumphantly. Our course is planned. The ship should take off in sixty seconds and take us to a landing pad on GU-T64A. He frowned at the screen a moment longer, then turned to Zbigu with a grim look on his face. In order to launch, we've got to disable the firsficld generator. It's doing something awful to my padscreen and I need to figure out how to calibrate and activate the bloodsucking blink. Get down there and turn the virus-ridden thing off before our company gets here.

"You couldn't have mentioned that earlier?" Zbigu threw up his hands and sent distracted acknowledgement before bolting down the ramp again. In the maelstrom of scents and noise outside the firsficld, he could hear the engineers' shouts already too close. Darting around the generator, he leapt up the steps and scanned the control panel, trying to figure out how on earth he was supposed to operate it.

He had been able to draw basic parallels to the ship innards and the cndrid technology before, as in Hirizcn he had studied both purely based on Scholar's lost curiosity, but the black and bulky generator was nothing like any of the generators he'd come into contact with before. He had limited time and no idea where to start, so he risked a brief, surface skim over the many humps and dips of the void in the spaces of his mind. He didn't couldn't find any information on potentially unaffiliated generator technologies and even the act of skimming made the void pulse and tug at his frayed mental threads. His head spun and he had to lean against the generator and just breathe for a moment.

Thirty seconds! Huras called out as an engineer appeared and grabbed Zbigu's shoulder, talking rapidly and pulling him away from the firsficld generator. You've got to get that shield down!

Zbigu yanked himself free from the engineer and dove for the generator, half-hysterically remembering other times he all had had to evade capture because of a mission gone wrong. His mind was more than half caught up in holding himself tightly centered in the mindhome, so he brute forced the generator by slamming his hand on anything that looked even remotely close to a button. More unrelated memories bombarded him and he shook his head, trying to clear his vision.

Twenty seconds! Another engineer, this one larger, stronger, grabbed ahold of Zbigu's whole arm and tried to pin it, and he ended up kicking him in the groin to get away. He stumbled back and barely missed the first engineer, darting a few quick steps around and desperately pounding the last few buttons on the generator's main panel that he could see.

Earsplitting alarms sounded and he jumped backward, crashing into the purple firsficld as it flickered. The contact shocked him badly, much stronger than he'd thought it would, and he spasmed on the ground, all the breath jarred out of his lungs. The first engineer cried out and dragged him away, slamming something into the generator's control panel to deactivate the further flickering firsficld. He just caught Huras's cry of Blink countdown's activated! Zbigu, what's got you held up? over the raucous din.

He had ten seconds. Zbigu tried to wrench himself free one last time and stumble toward his last concrete hope of seeing the rest of himself again, but the plasma shock still had him and he couldn't coax anything but irregular jerks from his voluntary muscles.

A flash of horror shot through him and Zbigu had to frantically pull himself inward against reaching out into the void. He wasn't going to make it. Again, he mentally threw himself toward getting free and scrambling into the ship, but only his left arm moved and the engineer holding him wrapped his hands more firmly and hauled him away to what was bound to be the hospital rooms. No, no, no, it couldn't end like this.

Door's closing! Where the deathwaste are you, Zbigu? Huras's irritated face poked out of the ship's entrance and paled to horror when he saw the frustrated engineers and Zbigu being dragged farther and farther away.

He really wasn't going to make it. Despair flared in the mind-home and he fought it back desperately, mind whirring for a way, any way, to even remotely salvage the situation. His thoughts flew to Tzeldea's reasons for preventing them from returning and his own realizations about the implications of the rest of him still being alive.

No time to order his thoughts. Impulsively, Zbigu wet his lips and yelled over the alarms and the wind and the ship's engine and the shouting. Tell the rest of myself that I'm here and they can make a one-way trip if they commandeer another GU-T64A cndrid and ship! Make sure you take credit for any technology you reverse engineer from Tzeldea's civilization so it doesn't get traced back to them! Go, I can learn to live a life here.

You sure about this, kid? Huras shouted back, stance tense and half taking several steps onto the rapidly closing ship's ramp.

Yes! Control finally began to return to his muscles and he tried to get his legs under him, determined to try reunite with himself one last time.

Even through the wind and the tears that were clouding over his eyes, he saw Huras's hands jerk and his face make a complicated expression. He straightened, took the few steps back into the ship, and snapped an Cbian salute as the ramp rose the last few meters and sealed off the door. Live a good life, Zbigu! was the final thing he heard before the ship's engines blasted and shot it out into the atmosphere.

A bitter taste caught in his mouth as the exhaust fumes whirled in the gales around them and his final hope of reunion left him to eke out a living among a culture of strangers. He let himself sag completely, making the young engineer put him down and readjust his grip. Huras and the rest of himself were gone now, lost to the distance between the stars. He was just going to have to learn to live suspended in the darkness of the void.

Tzeldea ran out and knelt beside him, frantically checking him over and touching her forehead to his. He was pretty sure she was switching rapidly between Dawihcn and ancient English, but he only caught two words: Zbigu, wai?

A sense of irony washed over him and he chuckled, but his weak laugh turned to a cough. Why did anyone do anything? Turning his head and letting it flop where he could see her face, he reached out beyond the borders of the mindhome and said: "You told me everyone's greatest desire was to be fully and completely known. Can you blame me for trying to get back to the rest of myself?"

Distress swirled around him and Tzeldea pressed her hands against the border, light flaring and words sent with multiple half-coherent layers of meaning. "But would you pursue it at the cost of our secrecy and yourself? Zbigu, you should know that your soul cannot handle another confrontation with the void. Is Demaniwel's way so repulsive to you because I did not realize what you did not understand?"

Sensory input and the mindhome blurred together, and he wasn't sure whether he reached out internally or externally to clasp Tzeldea's hand. "I'm here now," he murmured, sending forgiveness to soothe her waves of distraught. "and I told Huras to claim he invented the blink if he wants to offer an alternative to Zilcn drives. No one should find here anymore."

Tears floated into the mindhome and Zbigu forced himself to once again face the possibility of living the rest of his life on the edge of the void. "And as for Demaniwel's way? Tzeldea, I'm willing to try."

Epilogue

He all huddled tightly together in the mindhome, clinging to his sleeves as had become habit so none of him could accidentally stumble and fall into the void. Only Quartermaster made a halfhearted attempt to listen to the quiet droning of the grief counselor, the rest focused inward and only occasionally glancing at Quartermaster's nudges about interpreting the grief counselor's face.

…we are here for you. If you need help, all you have to do is ask.

Leader clutched his physical arms harder and pressed his mental back deeper into the intertwined Bcqu clump, letting the others swallow him and block out the external condemning words.

"Should I answer?" Scholar asked, head buried in Artist's chest and his exhaustion weighing down all the currents of the mindhome. "It's been months and things are still no better."

He all looked at him. Leader ducked his shoulders in further. "Do whatever you want," he sighed, same as the last fourteen times he had been asked. "Clearly my judgment is flawed if it directly led to the death of myself."

"That's not true," Artist, protested, anger flaring and arm tightening around Leader, as he had done fourteen times before. "It was the deathwasted freelancer's fault. He was the one who caused the cndrid to activate somehow!"

Quartermaster shoved between them and clapped his hands loudly enough to echo in the mindhome. "Please, stop it! I can't bear to be fighting again. Leader, I know it is hard, but get over yourself. I am not qualified to interface with other minds. Without— Without Speaker, you're the only part of me that knows how. I can't do this. Scholar and I can't keep doing this."

Leader's despair mixed in with Quartermaster's turmoil, weighing him further into his depression. He might be the only one qualified, but how could any part of him trust his own choices after that disastrous mission? He had been too confident and deliberately ignored Speaker's concerns, and now the mindhome had cracks that would run deep and compromise his own foundations for the rest of his day-cycles.

A notification blipped against his uniform, startling him all back into the physical world. Curiosity piqued and grasping for a non-emotional distraction, he all reached for the padscreen and entered his biometrics, keeping in synchrony to assuage the constant ache Speaker's absence left in his proprioception.

It was an unofficial notice, one of the routines Scholar and Quartermaster had coded in the main systems in a feverish attempt to deny the hole in the mindhome. Urgency: 5A. Danger level: 9C. Hirizcn class 3XC explorer kit distress signal detected at planet GU-T64A.

Pure shock jolted through his all systems, whiting out his sensory input for a moment. Scholar spoke first, thought breathless and unfinished. "That's the kit we left for—"

He all shared internal and external looks and bolted, sending his folding chairs flying and sprinting toward the launching bay. The grief counselor cried out behind him, but he spent no energy on the thought. All his focus was honed into synchrony in the purest form, thoughts so unanimous no one even verbalized them.

He sped round the corner, briefly breaking synchrony to dodge around a few startled employees. He glanced over and discarded the elevator— Too slow. Every moment counted. Wrenching the fire safety door open and turning another hairpin corner, he thundered up the stairs, noting and blocking out the mind-numbing cacophony of his footsteps. Blue and grey, floor after floor flew by in a blur. He barely acknowledged the increasing burning in his calves.

Floor 0. He burst through the airlock with his senior explorer's ID and made a beeline for the closest equivalent to his personal ship, breaking synchrony again to check it over and begin launching procedures as quickly as possible.

"Is the cargo clear?" Leader asked as he powered on the ship's controls and began to warm up the engine, shoving calculations at Quartermaster for the absolute fastest activation and exit routes possible without waiting for the usual space control clearance.

Scholar and Artist gave mental affirmation and sent their perspectives of the hold: half information updates, reports, and an entire portable med evacuation station for if Speaker was alive, and half real and fabricated blackmail and high-powered illegal weaponry for if he was not.

"Strap in," he called as Quartermaster's calculations spun out in the mindhome: with a little risky flying and immediate transition to 1st-level dimensional rift after the halfway point to avoid Zilcn drive disruption, they could arrive at GU-T64A within six hours and twenty-five minutes. In the background he felt Scholar buckle in his last strap and begin loading his padscreen routines to pinpoint the exact distress ping location and optimize it for fastest transmission before they entered interdimensional space.

He cast off and Artist wove around the traffic within moments until they were clear of the headquarters' asteroid and could enter dimensional rift. The journey there was spent in silence, tension so great that it was all he all could do to avoid injuring himself through anticipatory fidgeting. Quartermaster crunched and recrunched the calculations, even pulling Scholar in to help, but they had already chosen the fastest course and nothing could be done to shave off the distance even more.

The Zilcn drive sputtered around hour three, causing a round of acute frustration and an argument so intense it nearly devolved into a physical wrestling match. Artist eventually convinced him all to change angles slightly and jump into 2nd-level dimensional rift, but mercifully after that there were no more travel complications.

He exited dimensional rift at seven hours thirteen minutes and took sixty seconds more to circle the planet and hone in on the barely visible half clearing that the distress signal was coming from. Scholar and Quartermaster got out the poison tasers while Leader ran the final calculations for Artist's piloting. The scanners only detected one humanoid heat signature in the clearing, and it was the red-haired freelancer waving at them in sodden orange robes, not Speaker.

Cold fury tightened the knuckles of all his hands, and Leader accepted a poison taser of his own. The door hissed open and he shot out in synchrony, flinging the improvised gun out of the engineer's hands and pinning him to the ground with tasers primed and ready, Leader leaning down to scream out all his stored up anger into the freelancer's face. Where am I?!

Gah! Don't set your ship's drive to the wrong dimension, the murdering freelancer gasped, squirming fruitlessly for a few seconds before giving up and settling on rolling his eyes at him, as if his situation was a mere inconvenience. The other part of you's alive and well, just way too far out of reach. Hey, don't poke at me with that! He asked me to give a message to you all, and I'm not going to do that if you can't restrain yourselves to at least basic courtesy.

Artist's eyes widened and his taser nearly slipped out of his hands. "Speaker's alive?!"

Leader quivered with the force of the emotions racing through him, but he mentally shoved the decision to Scholar and Quartermaster. He was nowhere near a reliable decisionmaker in his current state, and all he wanted right now was to move his taser to the torture setting and dig it deep into the freelancer's high-handed, self-righteous gut.

Quartermaster and Scholar sent each other a flurry of nonverbal communication before stepping back in unison and allowing the freelancer to sit up and rub his arms. Upon prompting, Artist readjusted his grip, moved behind him, and lit his taser with a deliberate minor shock.

The freelancer yelped and twisted away, glaring, but when Leader shifted his hands on his own taser's grip he hastily cleared his throat and started speaking again. Alright, alright, listen. Your guy is fine, just stranded 10,000 years away. I was too, but I managed to escape. I hacked another old ship capable of the journey back that way. He jabbed a thumb toward the city ruins. If you give me your ship I'll let you take mine and head back to Speaker. Just know it's a one-way trip.

"How did he know what to call me?" Quartermaster hissed, conceiving and discarding scenarios faster than even Leader could track while occupied with his own reactions. "He must— It sounds farfetched but I don't see how he could determine my internal roles without one of my input. What does the rest of me think?"

Leader kept his physical body tense and focused on the engineer so he could not escape in any distraction he caused. His own anger mixed and curdled with Scholar's suspicion and Artist's desperate hope. This decision should not be in his hands. "I don't know. What does he mean by a ship capable of the journey? One run by one of those incomprehensible cndrids?"

Scholar sent agreement and a short nod into the rest of the mindhome. "Verbalize."

Leader gritted his teeth and repeated himself, wondering if the wretched freelancer even realized he had been the one to speak to him all those months ago. What do you mean exactly by "capable of the journey"?

The freelancer rolled his shoulders and settled back on his hands, casting a wary glance at Artist, who was still brandishing his taser, albeit weakly. Long story short, this ancient civilization is an isolationist bunch of secret hoarders and they invented an alternate, longer distance version of non-FTL space travel. Speaker and I got stranded and I managed to escape, but he decided to stay and make nice with his new friends. He told me to tell you he's alive and waiting for you if you also want to make the one-way trip out to see.

"We should go." Artist wrung his hands in the mindhome, disconnecting himself from mental touch for the first time since the separation. "I'm out there, waiting for me."

"I don't think he fabricated the story," Quartermaster said, fisting his hand tighter into Leader's mental shirt. "But do we really think Speaker is still alive? Surely even 10,000 light years away I would not see myself as a void in the mindhome."

Scholar quietly brought up a memory of a Hirizcn briefing on space travel. He all stared at the time fuzzed memory and the warning that had been written at the bottom of the page: Partial entry into dimensional rift may induce forced mental separation or even death.

Leader shuddered and turned his gaze away from the dark wound he all had reflexively turned to look at. Almost against his will, the different possibilities hovered in his focus and he weighed them: duty to Hirizcn versus reuniting with Speaker. The choice was obvious and he spoke impulsively, grabbing a fistful of the freelancer's robes and leaning in nose to nose before conferring with the rest of the mindhome. How do you activate the blink?

The engineer growled and pried uselessly at the grip in his fingers. You just power on the ship and begin to leave atmosphere, but—

He threw his taser on the ground and turned to the rest of himself, speaking without letting his lost self-confidence cripple him. "Let's go." Artist cheered, Quartermaster nodded, and Scholar cracked a long-absent smile, and he all slid into synchrony and sped into the rainforest, dropping his weapons and reconfiguring his sensors for unidentified large objects as he went.

Hey, wait, aren't you going to take any supplies— The engineer's shouts behind him were drowned out by his uncaringly reckless demolition of the local bioflora and his singular focus on the newly spotted goal.

The ship that would take him to Speaker was perched on a flat, mostly empty platform made of the ancient civilization's ubiquitous yellow stone. It was rounded and curiously streamlined for its purported range in space travel, but the door was already open and that was all he needed.

Leaping the last few steps, Leader was the first to pass through the firsficld covering the entrance and locate the ship's cockpit. An unassuming squarish cndrid was plugged into the dashboard, which was sparsely marked so that it was easy for him to locate the appropriate power button.

He slammed his hand on the indentation as soon as the rest of him was inside and the cndrid lit up in the cheerful red that had spelled the end of Speaker's life. But if the engineer's words were correct, that would not be true anymore. All his emotions twisted together in the mindhome, knotting and intertwining until pure adrenaline was all he could identify. He hadn't asked the freelancer about any of the travel time, so he had no estimate, but in as short as a few more moments, he could really find Speaker and be whole again.

He all pressed around the pilot's seat, attempting to wedge himself safely in the cockpit in lieu of having enough chairs and seatbelts, eyes fixed on the cndrid as it beeped several times and began to steer him out of atmosphere. His hearts pounded in his ears, emotions pulsing and half-verbalized thoughts colliding, a vivid image of surrounding Speaker and mentally surging around him as he slid back into the mindhome taking front and center. Leader joined hands with the rest of himself in taut anticipation as planet GU-T64A dropped away beneath them and the cndrid's automated voice piped up:

Beginning countdown to blink: 5, 4, 3, 2, 1.